S.T.A.R. FLIGHT

The Kaltich invaders are cruelly pro-longing their Earthmen serfs' lives and denying them the secret of instantaneous space travel, so desperately needed by a barbaric, overpopulated Earth. While the Kaltichs strip Earth of its riches, the Secret Terran Armed Resistance movement, STAR, opposes them — but it's only their agent, Martin Preston, who can possibly steal the aliens' secrets. If he fails, billions of people will starve — with no place to go to except to their graves.

E. C. TUBB

S.T.A.R. FLIGHT

Complete and Unabridged

LINFORD
Leicester

First published in Great Britain

First Linford Edition
published 2010

British Library CIP Data

Tubb, E. C.
    S.T.A.R. flight. - - (Linford mystery library)
    1. Space warfare- -Fiction. 2. Science fiction.
    3. Large type books.
    I. Title II. Series
    823.9′14–dc22

    ISBN 978–1–44480–497–3

Published by
F. A. Thorpe (Publishing)
Anstey, Leicestershire

Set by Words & Graphics Ltd.
Anstey, Leicestershire
Printed and bound in Great Britain by
T. J. International Ltd., Padstow, Cornwall

This book is printed on acid-free paper

To
Terry

1

Martin Preston opened his eyes and stared at a vaulted ceiling of natural stone. Through a mullioned window bright sunshine threw a pattern of lines and splotches over the high mound of the coverlet. Somewhere a bird twittered and, from below, came the harsh crunch of booted feet. Sentries, he thought and, suddenly, was wide awake.

Stretching, he looked about the room. It was small, bare, gay only with fabrics but it was in the Schloss Steyr with all that implied. He stretched again. The bed was soft, the coverlet made of genuine eiderdown, the sun bright on archaic furnishings.

He rose, showered in a small annex, not noticing the anachronism, shaved and combed his hair. The organizers had made things easy. He wore his own shirt, pants and shoes, slipping ornamented covers over the footwear, covering his twenty-first century clothes with a long robe with its girdle and jeweled dagger. He drew it. The blade was polished but of soft metal. He could, he supposed, do some damage with a really vicious thrust and would be able to cut butter if he had to but it was more of an ornament than a weapon. Lastly he donned the hat, a fore-and-aft affair with a feather.

After breakfast he examined the schloss.

Once there had been banners, trumpets, and full panoply of rank and privilege with armed and armoured men bristling like cockerels fiercely jealous of their pride. But that, thought Preston sadly, had been a long time ago. A time when the stars had been lanterns carried by angels to light the paths of souls to Heaven instead of the luminaries of habitable worlds. Now, though there were still banners and men carrying arms; tall halberdiers and those who, like himself, wore costume, it was a thing of make-believe; the pride that of those engaged in a successful business venture. Somehow it was not the same.

Outside, with the sun warm on his back and shoulders, he looked at the ancient, lichened stone of the schloss. Once that stone had given adequate protection to those within; the stone and the great portcullis which was ceremoniously lowered each evening at dusk. But that too was make-believe — a postern gave uninterrupted access to the hotel.

Turning, he filled his lungs with the clean mountain air. It carried the scent of pine from what remained of the forest below. Looking at the scanty trees it was hard to realize that when this castle was new, later even, the forest had stretched further than the eye could see. There had been wildlife, too — wolves, boars and smaller game. Bears too, perhaps. He must remember to ask.

'Good morning, Herr Preston.' The man was small, round, wearing the tabard of a herald. 'You are enjoying your holiday?'

Preston nodded. 'What little I've had of it.'

'Ah, you arrived but late yesterday — now I remember.' The herald spoke a curiously stilted Galactic. It was obviously an attempt to stay in character but,

3

thought Preston, to have done the job properly he should have used Latin or Norman French or some other forgotten tongue. But then, he asked himself, who would have been able to understand him?

'You slept well,' said the herald. 'All who come here sleep well. The air,' he touched the tips of bent fingers to his lips before throwing them to the horizon, 'is superb!'

Preston could agree with that. He hadn't slept so soundly or eaten breakfast with such an appetite for years.

'I come to announce the Great Tourney,' said the little man importantly. 'Late this afternoon knights will joust for the love of their ladies and the honour of their coat armour. There — '

'What is coat armour?' interrupted Preston.

'You see this?' The herald gestured towards his tabard. 'In the old days, ordinary people, you understand, could not read. And, when in armour, the face of the man could not be seen. But all could recognize symbols. So a knight wore certain devices on his shield and

4

surcoat to identify himself. Coat armour came to mean the badge of himself or his House. You understand?'

Preston nodded.

'There will be prizes,' continued the herald. 'Wagers may be laid. There will be refreshments and a Great Melee. And there will be real horses,' he added. 'Especially bred and flown in for the occasion. No expense has been spared to make this a unique spectacle. It is one you should not miss.'

'I don't intend to,' said Preston. He'd heard about these jousts. Not only real horses but real armour and weapons were used. There was real blood and some-times real death. Watching the carnage made the girls excited, erotic and eager for romance. Tonight, with luck, he wouldn't sleep alone.

'You are wise,' said the herald. 'Late this afternoon, remember. A ticket may be purchased from reception. It would be best not to delay.'

He nodded and moved on, a colourful little figure working hard to maintain an illusion. Preston watched him go, then entered the castle.

Inside were still ancient stones and stained arches, narrow, spiral stairs and wedge-shaped embrasures ending in cruciform arrow-slits. Even the cracked paving stones belonged to the distant past. But now they were covered with a layer of clear plastic, the once-ubiquitous dampness had been dried from the air, the natural gloom dissipated by strategically placed flambeaux. Colourful synthetics had replaced the tapestries which had once striven to soften the bleak walls. Burnished steel made spots of glitter against the stone.

Preston had an interest in weapons. He studied them, feeling a trace of envy for the soldiers of ancient times. Life had been much simpler then and war a personal thing. A man had to really be a man in those days, he thought. It was him against his opponent and no dodging. No hiding either. No running, what with wearing blazons of identity. There had to be pride then, he told himself. Pride of position. Pride in the symbols you wore. Above all pride of self. Pride, he thought.

A devalued word in the currency of today.

The armour was like a mirror, reflecting his face in distorted lines but not so distorted that it was grotesque. It was a strong face, hard, the eyes a little too deep, the mouth a little too thin. A young face prematurely aged by strain and responsibility.

Another joined it, smoother, softer, stamped with arrogance.

'You are interested in old things?' The Kaltich stood so close that Preston could smell the scent he wore, an acrid, orange-like perfume, hear the slight metallic sounds as he moved the arm from which dangled his whip.

Immediately he turned to face the alien. 'Yes, sire.'

'It is a tendency I have noted,' mused the Kaltich. He was old, the skin around his eyes creped with faint lines, corpulent beneath the wide belt he wore. He was dressed all in yellow and black. A beta, thought Preston. Probably an officer in charge of the blacks. 'You people seem to be enamored with the past. Even this,' he gestured with his whip at the hotel, 'is symptomatic. Why do you go to such trouble to recreate an ancient way of life?'

'As a diversion,' said Preston. 'As a novelty. It is something different,' he explained. 'People like to dress in exotic clothes and share a party atmosphere. It doesn't mean anything,' he added. 'It is only for amusement.'

'And the men who will try to kill each other this afternoon?'

'That too,' insisted Preston.

'An odd form of amusement. The watchers I can understand. The participants I cannot. They do it for reward?'

'There are prizes,' admitted Preston.

'But not for all?'

'No, sire. Only for those who win.'

The alien twitched his whip. Preston watched it with a cautious eye. The thing was an eighteen-inch length of woven metal, the whole covered with minute barbs carrying a particularly painful form of nerve-poison. A man could never forget having been struck with such a whip.

'I assure you, sire,' he said, 'it is so.'

The Kaltich made no comment. He

8

was, thought Preston, new to Earth. New and a little curious and probably more than a little suspicious. He felt a wave of anger. To hell with him! If he didn't like the way Earth lived he could leave. They could all leave, the whole supercilious bunch. We can do without them, he told himself. They and their ways and nasty little habits. Their insistence on a respectful form of address and their quickness to whip anyone who forgets. But, he thought bleakly, were they wholly to blame?

'I must congratulate you,' said the alien abruptly. 'Your Galactic is faultless.'

'Thank you, sire,' said Preston. 'For many years now it has been taught in all our schools.'

'That is wise,' said the Kaltich. 'Such enterprise is to be encouraged. It is important that you people should be able to communicate with those who live on other worlds. It will not be long,' he added, 'before you will be meeting them face to face.'

'We live for the day, sire,' said Preston tightly. He wondered if his rage was obvious. 'It seems a long time in coming.'

'It will come.' Again the twitch of the whip. 'When you are ready, it will come.'

And so, thought Preston savagely, will Christmas, free longevity for all, pie in the sky and a mule and forty acres for every man. Promises, he told himself. I'm sick of their damned promises. They've fed them to us for fifty years. We've lapped them up since they came among us from nowhere and made our own space programme seem like the pathetic efforts of children. We should have kept on, he thought. No matter how silly those rockets seemed. At least they would have been ours. We wouldn't have had to wait, begging, in the hope of being permitted to use their Celestial Gates. Wait and fall over backwards in trying to please them. We shouldn't have had to throw away our pride.

'You are attending the tourney this afternoon.' The Kaltich was abrupt. 'I shall require you to explain any detail of which I may not have knowledge. Arrange it.'

He strode away without waiting for a reply.

Fuming, Preston made his way to reception. He had looked forward to the tourney but now the enjoyment was gone. And so, he thought bitterly, was his vacation. Having found himself a convenient guide in Preston, the alien wouldn't bother to find another. Preston could refuse and possibly nothing would happen if he stayed out of the alien's way. But, in years to come, when he had need of what they offered, he would be refused. The Kaltich were never successfully opposed. Men valued life too highly for that.

'Yes, sir?' The girl behind the counter was young, lovely, more than beautiful in her robe of surrogate samite. Thick coils of hair were looped beneath a long, pointed hat from which trailed a veil of gossamer.

'I was talking to an alien,' said Preston hopefully. 'A beta. How long is he staying?'

'Cee Thurgood,' she said promptly. 'He is the only one we have staying with us,' she added. 'He is here for two weeks.'

Preston was booked for one. 'I want a ticket to the tourney,' he said dully. It was going to be a pretty grim week.

'A ticket to the joust? Certainly, sir.' Her smile was radiant. 'Your name?' He told her. Thoughtfully she pursed her lips. 'I believe there was a message for you, sir. Have you received it?'

'No.'

'It was sent to your room. A moment, if you please.' She went to a rack, returned with an envelope. 'Your pardon, sir. You were to have been paged.'

He took the envelope, ripped it open, read the message. It had originated in New York and consisted of two worlds. *Lewis Carroll*.

'Damn!' The transition was too abrupt. He had adjusted his mind to the prospect of an uninterrupted vacation, prepared to sink into the make-believe world of the castle. It had been the first chance to enjoy himself for years. He crumpled the scrap of paper in his fist.

'Is something wrong, sir?' The girl was concerned.

'Bad news,' he said. 'I'm afraid that I'll have to cancel my booking. Can that be arranged?'

She was dubious. 'It isn't normal sir. I don't know if a refund can be granted. The schloss is full and we don't accept short bookings.'

'Look,' he urged. 'I'm not going to be eating anything for the rest of the week. Not here. Can't I at least be refunded the value of the food?'

'I really don't know,' she insisted. 'The decision isn't mine to make. I'll ask the manager, but — '

'You do that,' he interrupted. 'Later. In the meantime is there a flight to New York this morning?' He brooded as she went to find out. The message was obvious when you knew the code. Carroll, his story and, more particularly, his poem.

'*The time has come, the walrus said, to speak of many things . . .* '

It was Raleigh who wanted to speak, of course, not the walrus. Preston wondered what the local chief of STAR had on his mind. Something important or he would never have been sent for. *The time has come!*

He dropped the message into his pocket as the girl returned.

'There is no direct flight this morning, sir.' She paused and Preston felt a guilty satisfaction. If he couldn't get away then it wouldn't be his fault. 'However, there is an ICPM leaving Salzburg for New York within the hour. If you hurry you will just be able to catch the local flight to the field. Shall I book you a place?'

'Do that,' said Preston. And ran upstairs to change.

2

There was trouble in the city. Preston sat glowering as the cab made yet another detour. He was tense, irritable, head and body aching from the punishing thrust of the rocket which had flung him six thousand miles in distance and six hours backwards in solar time. Intercontinental passenger missiles were all right, he thought, as long as you didn't have to ride in them. It was an experience he didn't want to repeat. And, after the schloss, New York smelt like a sewer. Even at five in the morning it stank. The city, he thought, was rapidly becoming nothing more than a festering abscess. Someone should lance it and soon.

He grunted with impatience as the cab braked to a halt. Leaning forward, he yelled through the partition. 'What's it this time?'

'A roadblock.' The driver was phlegmatic. You couldn't be anything else if you drove in the city and hoped to remain sane. 'Relax, buddy. It can't hold us up forever.'

Preston slumped back in his seat.

'You know,' said the driver, 'that's the trouble with the world. Too many guys in a hurry. And for what? To get somewhere fast. And what do they do when they get there? They sit down and beef about how long it took them. Now, what I say is if they didn't take time out to gripe they wouldn't have to be in such a hurry. Like the man said; what's the point of saving a coupla minutes if you don't know what you're going to do with them?'

Preston made noises, looking through the window at a red glow in the sky.

'Fire,' said the driver. 'All the time now we get fires. Like I was reading once, someone must be flame-happy. A piro . . . paro . . .'

'Pyromaniac,' said Preston.

'That's the word. Some guy just loves the sight of a good fire. A frustrated fire-man, maybe? What do you think, bud?'

'How long do you think we're going to be stuck here?'

'So who cares? An hour, a day, what's the difference? Listen,' said the cab driver. 'You got all the time in the world. We both have. You know all that three score and ten crap? Well, that's just for the birds. We got plenty of time. So why not sit back and enjoy yourself? You want music?' He thumbed the button of a radio. 'You got music. You want something to eat? That I can't give you. You want to stop feeling hungry? Just think of all those kids starving in the east. Anything else?'

'Yes,' said Preson. 'How much do I owe you?'

'You figuring on getting out, buddy? Here?'

'That's right.'

'Man, you're crazy!' The driver shook his head. 'The gangs are out and on the rampage. What do you think this holdup's for? You wanna get chased? Beaten to a jelly? Robbed and maybe killed? Take my advice, buddy, you sit it out and stay safe. So what if it costs a little? What's dough against skin? This heap's got shatterproof glass and locked doors. They may be able

17

to dent us a little, sure, but that's all they can do. Solid tyres, armoured gas tank, sealed hood. Man, we're impregnable!'

'How much,' said Preston tiredly. 'For the ride,' he added. 'I don't figure on paying for anything else.'

'Fifteen,' said the driver. He saw Preston's face. 'All right,' he corrected hastily. 'Just give me a fin.' He tripped the door lock as Preston handed him five gu's. 'Luck buddy. Watch yourself.' He slammed the door as Preston left the cab.

For the first half-mile there was no trouble. Rounding a corner, Preston saw a crowd and ducked back quickly before he was seen. Crossing the street, he ran the opposite way towards the glow of the fire. There would be police there and firemen. Soldiers too, perhaps. He turned another corner and ran smack into a group.

'Hey there, man! Lookit what we got!' A youth hair roached and dyed, naked but for moccasins, beads and a leather belt supporting an apron front and rear, jumped forward and gripped Preston by the arm. His other hand rested on the hilt of a knife tucked in his belt. 'A square!' he yelled. 'A regular square!'

'Gimmealook!' A girl, tall, lithe, young, breathed on Preston. She wore a loose, sleeveless dress, sandals, beads and a knife. Long plaits hung over prominent breasts. Like the youth she was hideous with paint. 'Hey, man!' she shrieked. 'Howdylike?' She turned and flipped up the back of her dress. She wore nothing beneath.

'You're going to be scalped,' said the youth with roached hair. 'Scalped but good!'

'Let's do it for real.' Others joined the few around Preston. A pimply-faced character came up and spat in his face. A badge the size of a saucer dangled on his shaved chest: *No Trespass on Terra!* A girl clung to his arm. She wore her badge lower down: *Don't Meditate__Copulate!*

'Ransom,' she shrilled. 'How much can he pay?'

'Take it all,' yelled a voice from the back of the crowd. 'Strip him for the gauntlet.'

'Scalp him!'

'Skin him!'

'Use him for a target!'

'Who's for long pig?'

Preston breathed deeply as he heard the suggestions. These kids weren't playing. Their knives weren't toys. The paint they wore in emulation of the old Indians was put on for the same basic reason. They were on the warpath hunting for prey. He had fallen right into their lap.

He looked at the youth with the roached hair. He was grinning, his grip not as tight as it had been, confident that the press of numbers would hold Preston safe. The girl leaned against him on the other side, pointed fingernails an inch from his eyes. She had, he thought absently, a nice figure. Washed, she would be really attractive.

Something hit him in the rear. He turned, spinning from the threatening nails, jerking his arm free of the youth's grip. A bearded, filth-stained man of about twenty stood behind him. He wore what seemed to be a necklace of human ears around his neck and the pelt of a king-sized rat on his head. He carried a rusty pitchfork in both hands. He lifted it, aiming at the eyes, yelling as he jabbed it forward. Preston swung up one arm, knocking it upwards so that it passed over his head. The man swore. Preston kicked him in the groin.

He jumped forward as the man fell, springing over the writhing body, landing on both feet. He fronted a knife, a pair of slanting eyes and a badge reading *Up All Aliens!* He drove his fist into the centre of the badge, dodged the knife, hit at the neck with the stiffened edge of his palm. Slant eyes made a grunting noise and toppled to one side. Two others rushed at Preston, saw his expression and changed their minds. Instead they joined the crowd chasing him as he raced down the street. Cheering, screaming, baying like hounds, they ran after him as if they were huntsmen after a fox.

Head down, elbows tucked into his sides, he ran towards the fire.

It was near the Yonkers Gate, a small block of once high-priced apartments, long ago converted to a still high-priced slum, now wreathed in flame. The dispossessed stood about with a few hastily salvaged belongings. Hoses snaked from hydrants and a couple of helicopters were dropping oxygen-absorbing foam. Above the engines, the noise, the roar of flames could be heard the thin, spiteful sounds of shots. An armoured police truck swung up its dual machine guns and blasted a nearby rooftop. One of the helicopters swung low and robbed the place of breathable air. There were no more shots.

Preston skirted the fire, no longer running but still followed by the zanily dressed crowd. Somehow he had become the head of a yelling conga line. He led them towards the Gate where a triple line of armed soldiers stood on guard. The National Guard, he thought, or regular troops. They stood in a circle about the perimeter of the Gate and looked like they meant business.

'Hey, lookit the boy scouts!' The youth with the roached hair ran past Preston and thumbed his nose at the guards. The girl followed, turning and flipping up the back of her dress in unmistakable insult.

'Beat it,' snapped a guard. 'Quick or you'll get perforated.'

'Says who?' sneered the youth.

'Alien lover,' yelled the girl.

'I mean it,' said the guard. 'We got orders. Start shoving and you'll be sorry. Now get the hell out of here before you get hurt.'

He was on edge, sweating, the moisture running down his face from the inside of his helmet. His eyes were wild. The knuckles of both hands showed white where he gripped his gun. An automatic rifle, Preston noted. These boys were ready for anything.

Quietly he turned and walked away.

★　★　★

Off to one side a convoy of trucks stood with covered loads, the vehicles grouped in a tight echelon. Their drivers stood in a cluster, smoking, watching what was going on. Preston joined them and nodded towards the vehicles. 'Waiting to unload?'

One of the drivers took the cigarlet from his mouth. A number three size, Preston saw; driving for the Gates paid well. 'What's it to you?'

'Fifty if you can get me inside.' It was a hopeless request but it served as an excuse. The zanies were still milling around and he didn't want them to catch him alone. 'Fifty,' he said again. 'On!'

'You're crazy.' The driver was a big man with a mottled face and a wart on the side of his nose. 'So we put you in the truck and drive you up to the Gate,' he said. 'What happens when we unload?'

'You put me in a crate,' said Preston. 'Nail it tight. How are they going to know what's in it?'

'They check every item,' said another driver. He looked at Preston and shook his head. 'You wouldn't have a chance,' he insisted. 'They'd find you for sure.' He kicked thoughtfully at a tyre. 'You ever been beaten with one of those whips?'

Preston didn't answer.

'Once over the line, pal, and you're in Kaltich territory. They don't take kindly to trespassers. You get whipped and you'll wish that you'd never been born. Anyway,' he said, 'why do you want to get to the Gate? You thinking of passing through?'

'Maybe,' said Preston.

'Why? Isn't Earth good enough for you?'

'That's right,' said the driver with the wart on his nose. 'You on the run, buster?'

'No,' said Preston. 'It isn't that.'

'Then what's the idea of the bribe?' The driver glowered.

'Nothing,' said Preston. He began to walk away. 'I only asked,' he said. 'That's all.'

'You a spot? You testing our loyalty or something?' The driver spat out his cigarlet and lifted a clenched fist. 'Why, for two pins I'd — '

'Can it, Joe,' snapped the other driver. 'So it was a test. We passed, didn't we? So can it.'

'He was trying to bribe us,' said Joe. He sounded aggrieved. 'We should report it, turn him in.'

Nice, thought Preston. One of your

own kind, your own race, willing to do a thing like that. To tell an alien that you were trying to get close to his precious Gate. To open his big mouth and get you beaten and blacklisted and maybe worse. Scum like that isn't worth saving, he told himself. Let them rot in their own slime. But they aren't all like that, he thought. Maybe not even them, not really. It's just that they've got good jobs and don't want to lose them. But the rancour remained.

Earthmen, he thought, on their knees to the Kaltich. To hell with them.

He walked quickly from the Gate, the fire, the suspicious drivers. The zanies had gone, running wild through the streets, probably looking for fresh prey, more mischief, something to hurt or destroy. Kids, he thought. Still wet behind the ears but all the more vicious because of it. Kids with the motivations of adults and the thoughtless cruelty of children.

They're bored, he told himself. Kept too long at school and with nothing to do when they leave. No work, no place in society, nowhere decent to live. Just waiting, killing time until the Kaltich open the Celestial Gates. If they ever opened them. If they ever let the teeming billions of Earth through the empty worlds they swore were waiting.

And, thought Preston, in the meantime we wait, work, say yes, sire, no, sire, three bags full, sire. Eat dirt and grovel for the promise of what? Life, he admitted, that was real enough. The longevity shots they sold and which restored youth for a ten-year period. Spare parts for surgical implants. And the promise that, one day, they would open the Gates and give paradise to every man, woman and child on Earth.

One day.

Pie in the sky, he thought bitterly. Pie in the sky.

Close to the rendezvous he took care to make certain that he was not being followed. He doubted if anyone could have climbed on his tail but it was always possible. And so was something else. Carefully he checked his pockets. Keys, wallet, folding knife, money, pen, handkerchief, comb, cigarlets and lighter. His luggage was at the airport waiting later collection. The weather was too mild for topcoat or hat. He looked curiously at a small, flat, disc-like object he'd found in the top outer pocket of his jacket.

The girl, of course. She must have slipped it there while she threatened him with her nails. Now he came to think of it there had been nothing childish about her body. A UNO agent? It seemed like it. She would hardly belong to STAR. They would have no reason to load him with a bug.

Hefting it in his hand he stood, eyes shadowed with thought. To dump it? Keep it? Render it inoperative?

He looked around. He was standing before an old building made of brick. The mortar had crumbled leaving deep recesses. He located a place mark, counted, slipped the bug firmly into a crack low down close to the sidewalk. He would recover it later if he wanted. For now it would do no harm. It might even draw out whoever was tagging him.

He glanced at his watch. He had no time to linger. He was late as it was.

3

STAR had its New York special rendezvous in the cellar of a dilapidated
restaurant owned by a member of the
organization. Preston entered, walked to
the bar and ordered a drink. 'Lager.
Brunmilch Black Label.'

The bartender dumped bottle and glass
on the counter, opened the bottle and
took the money. He left the cap lying
beside the glass. Preston palmed it as he
picked up his drink. Sipping it he stared
over the restaurant.

Like most places it was open twenty-
four hours a day and, no matter what the
hour, there were always people eating,
drinking, courting, reading or just sitting
killing time. And always there was the
resident bar-philosopher.

'You got a light, pal?' He was thin with
a soiled shirt and tie, his face covered
with tiny red lines from broken capillaries. The stump of a number five cigarlet

hung from the corner of his mouth. 'Thanks,' He puffed smoke. 'You look intelligent,' he said. 'You look as if you could follow a line of reasoned argument. Name's Daler,' he said. 'Sam Daler.'

Preston touched the proffered hand.

'I was telling that creep behind the bar how to cure our problems,' said Daler. 'You know what they are? Too many people,' he said. 'That's the trouble with the world now. Too many goddamned people.'

Preston swallowed more of his lager.

'So what should we do about it?' said Daler. 'Kill 'em?' He shook his head. 'Can't do that,' he said with an alcoholic's concern with detail. 'That would be murder. We just can't kill 'em like a lot of vermin. No. You know what we should do?'

'Yes,' said Preston.

'You know?'

'Sure,' said Preston. 'Let them all die of old age.' He winced at Daler's roar of laughter.

'Say, that's good!' he yelled. 'That's real good!' He squinted at Preston's glass.

'Let's have a drink on that. You want another of the same?'

'No,' said Preston.

'Something else, then?'

Preston shook his head, finished his drink and walked from the bar. The toilets were upstairs. He reached them and looked behind. Nobody was watching. He passed the twin doors and ducked behind a curtain. It covered another, heavier door with a slotted box-lock. He slipped the bottle cap into the slot, waited three seconds, then pushed the door open. Beyond lay a flight of stairs leading to the cellar. At the foot was a door with a judas window. He knocked, waited, passed through as the door opened.

'You're late,' accused Oldsworth. He slammed and barred the door. 'We've been waiting. What held you up?'

'I ran into a bunch of zanies.' Preston told what had happened. 'I was also bugged,' he said mildly. 'Did it come from here?'

'Bugged?' Jim Raleigh turned white. 'Did you — '

'I dumped it,' explained Preston. 'I hid

it somewhere safe. Maybe we can find out who is interested in my movements. My guess is that the UNO is getting nosy. Maybe the whole thing was a mistake.' He walked to the table in the centre of the room and sat down. Deliberately he looked around.

Raleigh, the local chief, sat beside Oldsworth, who owned an electronics factory. He looked older than Preston remembered. He must be about due for another treatment, he thought. Jim too, no wonder he acted so scared. The third man was Bernard King, head of local security. The fourth person at the table was a woman.

'Hilda Thorenson,' she introduced herself. 'We haven't met. I'm a doctor.'

'Medicine, divinity or philosophy?'

'Medicine. I'm a surgeon. And you, of course are Martin Preston. One of STAR's best agents. Did you enjoy your vacation?'

'Sure,' he said. 'The whole seventeen hours of it.' Leaning back he lit a cigarlet and studied the woman. She had attractive, Nordic features and thick blonde hair. She also, thought Preston, had remarkably beautiful hands. 'While we're on the subject,' he said flatly. 'Someone owes me some money. You don't cancel bookings at the Schloss Steyr. You wanted me to get here in a hurry so you can make good the damage.'

'Money,' said Oldsworth. 'Is that all you think about? Money!'

'Now, Harry, take it easy.' Raleigh laid a soothing hand on Oldsworth's arm. 'Martin has a right to say what he did. But he doesn't mean it.'

'Think again,' said Preston coldly. 'Look,' he said. 'You're laughing. Oldsworth has his own business, you're something high up somewhere, King isn't exactly broke.' He looked at the woman. 'You're all right, doctors come high. What have I got?' He answered his own question. 'A half-share in a crummy debt collecting agency. Do you know how long it took me to save for that vacation?'

'Never mind,' said the woman. 'You'll get your money.'

'It's not just that,' he said, mollified. 'I had to bounce an alien.' He looked into their startled eyes. 'That's right. One of the Kaltich picked me to act as guide. I had to let him down. How much do I get paid for losing my chance at longevity?'

'Now really, Martin.' Oldsworth ran the tip of his tongue over his lips. He reminded Preston of a snake. 'You can hardly blame that on us. In any case,' he added hopefully, 'I doubt if he would remember you.'

'Talk sense.' Preston was irritated, the more so because the situation was of his own making. He had forgotten all about the alien until he was packed aboard the ICPM. At least he could have pleaded sick or something. 'He doesn't have to remember me. All he needs to do is to notify their computer and it's curtains for yours truly. Anyway,' he said. 'It's done now. What's the urgency?'

'This,' said King. He threw a box on the table. It slid along, stopping just before Preston. He opened it.

It contained a neatly severed pair of human hands.

* * *

'Lassiter,' said King. He had a broad, flat face which disguised all emotion. He could have been talking about the weather. 'I've checked the prints and there's no doubt about it.'

'How did you get them?' Preston didn't touch the contents of the box. They rested flaccid, pale pink on the palms, deep ebony the rest, strong, long-fingered, sensitive hands. Lassiter had liked to play the guitar and had been good at it. What was the point of a guitar player without hands? 'How did you get them?' he said again.

'You don't have to shout,' said Old-sworth.

'All right, Harry.' Again Raleigh quietened his friend, 'They were sent to UNO,' he explained. 'By normal post. We have contact there. One of them passed the box to me. To deliver,' he added. 'Lassiter has a sister.'

'Chloe.' Preston slammed the lid back on the box. 'You were going to give them to her?'

'No, of course not, but I had to let her know he was dead.'

'And when you'd done that, then what?'

'How do you mean?'

'What were you supposed to do with the hands?' Preston was impatient. 'Bury them? Cremate them? Hang them out to dry?'

'I was going to destroy them,' said Raleigh. 'In the furnace.'

'They don't want them back at UNO,' said King. 'If that's what you were getting at.'

Preston nodded and looked at the doctor. 'Have you examined them?'

'I have.'

'And?'

'They were very neatly removed,' she said clinically. 'There are no signs of crushing or bruising nor the slightest trace of compression. They certainly were never chopped off and the wounds are too even for them to have been removed by hand. Something like a microtome could have done it but that's about all.'

'And the rest of him?' Preston looked at the others, 'The rest of Lassiter?'

Raleigh shook his head. 'No one knows,' he admitted. 'We can only assume that he is dead. They must have discovered him,' he said. 'I knew the plan was stupid from the first. The Kaltich aren't that easily deceived.'

'What happened?'

'We managed to get him among a bunch of selectees,' said King heavily. 'It was his own idea. He reckoned he could make it. He intended to pass through, look around and find some way back so he could tell us what he'd seen.' He shrugged, broad face impassive. 'That's all. They must have discovered him in some way and killed him. Sending back his hands was just to let us know they knew about it. A warning.'

'Hands off,' said Preston. He looked at his own, clenched into fists. 'Damn them,' he said. 'The barbaric swine.' He looked at Raleigh. 'What is the UNO going to do about it?'

Raleigh shook his head.

'STAR, then?'

'That's why we sent for you.' Oldsworth coughed, shielding his mouth with a handkerchief. 'We've got to make a decision.'

Preston raised his eyebrows.

'Let's review the situation,' said Old-sworth. He was, Preston reminded himself, no fool. No man who had made his kind of money could be. 'You don't remember the Kaltich arriving,' he said. 'You weren't born then. It was fifty years ago back in 1983. I was seventy years old then and had a cancer of the spleen. I'll be honest — I was damned glad they'd come.'

'Sure,' said Preston. 'They sold you a new spleen. They sold you the longevity treatment and made you young again for another ten years. You,' he added, 'and everyone in your position. Hell, you begged them to give it to you. Gave the Kaltich everything they wanted. How do you like being a beggar, Oldsworth?'

'You're not being fair,' said Hilda Thorenson. 'You're young and can't appreciate the desperation of the old.'

'Think again,' he said curtly. 'I watched my grandfather die when a thousand lousy units would have saved him. Given him another ten years at least,' he qualified. 'I was eight at the time. Now I'm watching my old man go through the same hell. Only he doesn't have to worry,' he added. 'I've got his cash safely put to one side. He'll make it — if he hasn't upset the Kaltich in some way. Like I did,' he reminded them. 'I let one down in order to attend this meeting.'

'He didn't know you,' said Raleigh. 'He can't know who you are.'

'He could check. The schloss has my particulars.'

King cleared his throat. 'Maybe we could do something about that.'

Preston shook his head. 'It's too late for that.' And then, to Oldsworth. 'Sorry. For interrupting you, I mean.'

'That's all right,' said Oldsworth mildly. 'I guess you are right in what you say. We did go overboard for the Kaltich. They offered life. What more attractive bait could be dangled before the old? Life and youth both. Sure we took it. We still take it. We are still willing to beg. But that part is all wrong. We shouldn't have to do that.'

Preston lit a fresh cigarlet, blew smoke, watched as it hit the table to bounce in spreading mist. They want something, he thought. They asked me to come here with a prime-urgent message and now they're dodging the problem. Or perhaps they weren't dodging it. Perhaps they were being clever. He blew more smoke. Clever? He doubted it. King, perhaps, he was a born agent. Raleigh, maybe, he had to have something in order to be able to hold down two jobs, one on each of two opposing sides. The woman? Yes, but in a different way. Her skill was a thing of hands, brains and painstaking care. Oldsworth? He was the odd man out. The financier for the group. What did he have to gain?

'You sent for me,' he said abruptly. 'I'm here. What is it you want from me?'

'We want you to go through a Gate,' said the woman evenly. 'We want you to try.'

'And wind up like Lassiter?'

'No. There is danger,' she admitted. 'He failed; so could you, but maybe not.'

Preston dragged at the cigarlet. 'Tell me more.'

'The Kaltich have two great advantages over us,' she said. 'One we can do something about. Our own geriatric sciences could, in time, maybe manage to duplicate the longevity treatment. If so, we can nullify one of their advantages. The other we can do nothing about. We still need their Celestial Gates. As yet we haven't the faintest idea of how they work.'

'Must you state the obvious?'

'I wish to clarify the position,' she said sharply. 'In order to solve a problem you must first recognize it. STAR was born from resentment, anger, frustration, a desire of individuals to be a part of an active force in the world. Unity is strength. Lassiter forgot that. Did he imagine that he could win the secret of the Gates merely by passing through? Do you?'

'No,' said Preston, and added, 'Is that what you want?'

She was emphatic. 'It's what we all want, STAR, UNO, everyone. It's worth a million,' she said casually. 'One million in cash if you can win for us the secret of the Gates.'

'And?'

'Another million if you can discover the secret of the longevity treatment. STAR doesn't expect you to work for nothing,' she said. 'What do you say?'

Preston rose to his feet. 'Do I get out alive or do you gun me down as I reach the door?'

'You refuse?'

'I don't play a guitar,' he said. 'But I've got a use for my hands. Yes, I refuse.'

Oldsworth coughed, this time using a fresh handkerchief. It seemed as if his lungs were tearing loose from his chest. Preston looked at him.

'You'd better go for a treatment,' he suggested. 'Leave it much longer and you'll be too late. Even the Kaltich can't resurrect the dead.'

Oldsworth managed to get himself under control. 'I've been for a treatment. I was refused.'

'That's tough.' So that's why there're millions floating around, he thought. You've cheated the grave for fifty years. Now it stares you in the face. Now you're getting desperate. Desperate enough to take any kind of a risk as long as it's only a financial one. Preston felt disappointed, for a moment he'd imagined the old man had recovered his pride. 'Lassiter?'

'I don't know. He may have talked, we can't be certain. If he did most of us in this group are branded. He knew a lot of us,' said Oldsworth. 'You too,' he pointed out.

Preston shrugged.

'We have a plan,' said the woman suddenly. 'It won't just be a matter of going blindly into the unknown. We think that we can win.'

'Sure,' said Preston. 'You and Lassiter all over again. But it was his hands which came back, not yours.' He crossed to the door. 'Sorry. Get yourself another boy.'

'Call me if you change your mind,' she said. 'I'm in the book.'

*   *   *

Outside it was a bright day, though still early. Too early for the normal rush of morning commuters. A few hopeful derelicts wandered the streets, picking over the trash, looking for something they could turn into food and drink. A wagon drove past looking for any night-born dead. A zany, eyes glazed with dope,

43

staggered back to his pad.

Preston walked slowly to where he'd planted the bug. A casual walk past showed that it was still there. He checked the area for watchers but the place was clean. He lit a cigarlet and waited, hiding behind a paper he'd picked up, looking through a tiny hole punched in one of the pages. He was nothing. A man killing time. Someone waiting to start work, someone out of work, someone on his way home, lingering until it was time to go to his share of a communal bed.

He smoked five more cigarlets and was about to give up when the car arrived. It was a big, black-painted job, the rear compartment, hidden behind opaque windows. It stopped where he'd planted the instrument. A girl left the vehicle. She no longer wore a sleeveless dress, sandals and beads. She didn't even wear paint, at least not much, and he would have bet his life that she now wore underclothes. But he couldn't mistake her hips. They were clearly visible as she stooped, plucked out the bug and returned to the car.

4

Cherry Lee ducked her head as she entered the car and handed the bug to the man sitting in the rear compartment. Chung Hoo took it, looked at it, slowly shook his head. 'That wasn't very wise of you, my dear,' he said mildly. 'Now the young man must be suspicious.'

'I doubt it,' she said. She gasped as the car moved forward, the acceleration throwing her against the cushions. 'He can't know that it was I who planted it,' she insisted. 'Even though he found it he could only guess. He's smart,' she added, 'Not many men would think to search themselves before going to an illegal rendezvous.'

Chung Hoo made no comment. He sat, as bland and benign as a carved Buddha, the bug cradled in his hand. After a moment he looked at it and handed it back to the girl.

'Return this to the appropriate department,' he said. 'Have them check it. It could be faulty, which could be the reason he found it.'

He's trying to save my face, she thought. Blaming the instrument instead of me. But I didn't bungle it. I know I didn't. Even so he's sweet for being so considerate. Aloud she said, 'Shall I follow him?'

'Why bother?' He appraised her with his eyes. 'There is a better way. Get to know him. Get him to like you — that should not be hard. Maybe he'll trust you. You could even join STAR.'

'They are patriots,' he said mildly. 'They believe they are working for the good of Earth. They don't seem to understand that we cannot afford to alienate the Kaltich. We dare not.' He looked through the window as the car approached the UNO building. It looked like a slab of mottled, dirty glass. 'We are so close to universal peace,' he said more to himself than the girl. 'At last all nations are becoming one. The old frontiers are being swept aside. Passports, customs, tariff barriers, all are going. The new language and the new unit of currency are uniting us all. How foolish it seems to squabble over a scrap of ground when there are worlds without number waiting to be explored.'

'When?' she asked.

'I don't know,' he admitted. 'When we are ready.'

'And just what does that mean?'

'When we have outgrown the childish habit of forming secret societies,' he said. 'Groups such as the Secret Terian Armed Resistance. STAR is dangerous. They want freedom for Earth, Freedom from the Kaltich. They don't seem to realize that, but for our guests, Earth would be a smoking ruin. War was very close,' he explained. 'Fifty years ago it was only a matter of time before someone started Armageddon. There were enough nuclear devices in stock to completely vaporize the planet. I do not believe in the Christian concept of God,' he admitted. 'But certainly some greater power seemed to have our welfare at heart.'

'That is the past,' she said. 'Now there is no threat of war.'

'But there could be,' he said quickly. 'If

it were not for the Kaltich the old rivalries and jealousies would again spring to life. Fifty years is not long enough to weld a world into a composite whole. Another hundred years and perhaps we shall not need them. Now we do. That is why STAR is dangerous,' he explained. 'They may force our guests to leave. That is why you work among the zanies — turning them from the Gates when they seek to destroy. You and others.'

'Cogs in the machine,' she said. She could not appreciate his dream — but then, she thought, I didn't live in the old days, I didn't know what it was like. To wonder each day, she thought, if that day was to be the last. And Chung Hoo knew more than most. His position in UNO saw to that. As permanent secretary to the Secretary General he had more power than most supposed. To him the coming of the Kaltich must have seemed like the descent of angels.

'Cogs,' he said thoughtfully. 'Yes, my dear, you are correct. But what machine could work without its small but essential components? Therefore, my dear, you are more important than I.'

She sat, hands folded, not answering as the car reached the UNO building and dived down a ramp into the underground car park. She had never thought of herself in quite that way before.

* * *

Chung Hoo ate breakfast in the high-level canteen, a substantial meal of fruit juice, cereal, buckwheat toast, flapjacks and maple syrup with tea and a pipe of opium to follow. It was a large meal but he didn't feel guilty. He'd been on duty since two a.m., rising at the first news of the fire and disturbance, and this was his first meal of the day. He would eat once more during the twenty-four hour period, probably in eight hours time, and if he got to bed before midnight he would be lucky.

His secretary looked up from her desk as he entered his office. She was a pale, intense young woman from the European Federation, her hair drawn back in a hard bun, her face devoid of makeup. She practised yoga and thought of Chung as a modern saint.

'I was about to page you,' she said. 'You have a visitor. Sire Eldon of the Kaltich,' she added. 'I thought it best to pass him in.'

'Eldon? Not Kondor?'

'No, sir. This one is new.'

Chung thanked her and passed into his own, inner office. The alien was sitting at his desk. He was dressed all in green, a gamma, and Chung fought a momentary irritation. It was bad enough that the Kaltich had sent a stranger, to have sent a man of lower rank was a deliberate insult. He crushed the thought. You don't know that an insult was intended, he told himself. Don't confuse the mores of Earth with those of the Kaltich. And yet, after fifty years, he was not wholly ignorant of their ways.

'I am honoured, sire,' he said, approaching his visitor. 'To what do I owe this pleasure?'

'There was a fire last night close to the Celestial Gate,' said Eldon. 'A delivery of supplies was delayed because of it. This must not happen again.'

'We hope that it will not,' said Chung.

'If it does the Gate may be closed. It is incredible,' continued the alien, 'that you fail to appreciate the service we give you. In return we ask so little. This fire,' he said. 'Who started it? What was its cause?'

'Our young people are getting impatient,' said Chung. 'They are overcrowded, unemployed. If you could see fit to grant us access to a new world — ' He broke off. The alien wasn't listening. They are all the same, thought Chung, looking at the hard, white face. All arrogant, all giving the impression that they couldn't be bothered with the local problems of Earth. And, he told himself, they were probably justified. What was one world among so many? How many? He didn't know. No one did. No one but the Kaltich and they spoke of worlds as if they were grains of sand. 'We shall do our best to prevent a repetition of the trouble,' he said. 'We like it even less than you. You may rest — '

'There is another thing,' interrupted the alien. 'As from today the cost of our services will be doubled. You have no one to blame but yourselves,' he pointed out. 'The cost of the items we purchase from you has greatly increased since we first did business. It is only fair that the cost of our services should rise in proportion. I am sure, Mr Chung, you will agree with that.'

Inflation, thought Chung bleakly. A two-edged sword. 'These increases,' he said desperately. 'They will hit our people very hard. It is not possible for you to reconsider? A subsidy on all goods you purchase, perhaps?'

'As from midnight,' said the alien, not bothering to discuss the matter. 'It would be best for you to broadcast the information. You understand?'

'Yes, sire.'

'That will be all.'

And that, Chung thought, looking after his departing visitor, was more than enough. He pressed a button on his intercom. 'Nader? Chung. Get up here and fast!'

Nader was the head of the UNO information service. He sucked in his cheeks at the news and savagely kicked a wastepaper basket. 'It isn't going to be easy,' he said, 'How the hell can we justify it? The economy is breaking at the seams already. How do I put it over?'

'Play up the survival aspect,' suggested Chung. 'Get the youngsters to start their longevity fund right away. Tread on the smoking, drinking, drug habits. Make them appreciate that saving is all-important.'

'*Don't Fritter Away Your Lives!*' mused Nader. He shook his head: the slogan lacked punch. 'It's going to play hell with the consumer industries,' he pointed out. 'The governments too. Those things carry high taxes. We'll have opposition.'

'Maybe, but you know how to handle it.'

'Sure. I can use surrogate artifacts, men and women, boys and girls, hit the sex angle and play up the pioneer spirit. We can even hint that this is the final stage before moving to our new worlds.' Nader hesitated. 'I don't suppose there could be any truth in that? I mean, did that louse say anything about letting us through?'

Chung shook his head.

'I didn't think so,' said Nader disgustedly. He looked at his hands. 'Maybe STAR has the right idea,' he murmured. 'Maybe we've forgotten that to act like a doormat is to be treated like one.'

'We must trust the Kaltich,' said Chung sharply.

'Maybe. But maybe we're just wasting our time.'

'No,' said Chung. 'I can't believe that.' I can't believe it because I dare not, he thought. And then, to Nader, 'Get on with the presentation right away. World coverage. The new prices start at midnight so we haven't much time.'

Nader left the office, scowling, a jumble of thoughts in his head. I'll have to use a full crew, he thought, and they can like the overtime or lump it. There's no time to have special surrogates made; we'll have to use those we've got together with every other trick in stock. Actors, he thought, then decided against it. It would be best not to use outsiders for fear of leaking the news. A before-and-after effect, he told himself. Something with lots of sex-appeal. An old woman suddenly turning into a ravishingly beautiful young girl. Not too suddenly, he corrected. Stretch the suspension, aim for the big build-up, hit them with the bad while they were entranced by the good. But still a beautiful girl. Cherry Lee, he decided. She would be ideal. He'd have to see if she was in the building.

★ ★ ★

As a rush production it was quite good. William Preston looked at the television screen as he ate a late lunch of soy bean soup, noodles, algae bread and Brazilian coffee. Beside him Ed Lever made slobbering noises over his bowl. A pig, thought Preston irritably. So Ed was old, but did he have to make such a sound-production out of a simple meal? He ate the last of his bread and drained his cup of coffee. Before him the screen swirled with colour turning the ten-by-ten utiliflat into an Aladdin's Cave of glowing splendour.

Ed sucked loudly at the last of his soup.

'For Pete's sake!' Preston slammed down his cup. 'Do you have to make such a noise?'

'It's my teeth,' whined Ed. He was on charity and wanted to please. 'They don't fit so good.'

'Then get some new ones,' said Preston. He'd known Ed for ten years but a thing like that could strain friendship to the breaking point. Beside him Ed sniffed.

'It's easy for you to talk,' he said. 'You've got a good boy in Martin. He lets you live with him. He pays for all you need. Me? I ain't got no one. It's easy for you to talk,' he repeated. 'But new teeth cost money.'

'Shut up,' said Preston. He felt a touch of guilt. What Ed had said was true enough. But, he thought fiercely, I'm not sponging on Martin. I do what I can and eat as little as possible. If there was work available I'd do it. He knows that. 'Here,' he said, and threw Ed a number four size cigarlet. 'Suck on this and let me concentrate.'

'Thanks.' Ed inhaled with a noisy

rasping. 'Didn't you used to work on television?'

'Advertising.' Preston kept his eyes glued to the screen. 'Now pipe down!'

The swirl of colour solidified, took shape as the background music faded, became the handsome, serious face of a middle-aged man.

'People of the world!' he said. 'An important announcement! Now! At last! The new longevity treatment as offered by our friends the Kaltich. To you all on this lucky day we bring the news. For only a little higher cost you too can enjoy endless, exhilarating, wonderful youth!'

Preston sniffed. The old buildup, he thought. Tell them it's new. Drive home the fact that it's bigger, better, brighter than ever before. Sell the product as something startling. A new package, he thought, but the same old contents. Cynical, he could still appreciate the expert skill behind the production.

'This is how it is done,' said the man. His face dissolved, was replaced by a spartan, hospital-like interior. A line of old people sat on a bench against a wall.

57

A man in a green coat turned as the camera zoomed in on his face. He was smiling, benign. Behind him, subtly out of focus, loomed the expanse of a gigantic machine; a wall of dials, lights and coloured tabs.

'If a thing lacks colour,' murmured Preston, rememberring, 'put it in.'

'Be quiet,' said Ed.

' . . . grow old, age and finally die,' the man in the green coat was saying. 'All you young people need to do to prove this is to look around. But, because of the Kaltich, no one now need be old. Watch!'

The scene widened. An old woman hobbled from the bench to where the man in the green coat was standing. Her eyes were sunken, her back bowed, knotted varicose veins showed like blue snakes on legs and arms. She seemed to smell of decay.

'First,' said the doctor, 'we test for organic malfunction. If a heart is diseased,' he explained, 'or lungs rotted with cancer, these organs must first be replaced. A simple check will determine what is needed.' He attached wires to the stooped figure of the crone. 'She is fortunate,' he said. 'Replacements will not be necessary. However,' his face loomed huge, no longer smiling, the voice deadly serious, 'you can see how important it is that you safeguard your health. Do not leave the rejuvenation treatment until the last possible moment.'

'That's it,' said Preston. 'That's the new product. From now on they'll call it the rejuvenation treatment. You see.'

Ed said nothing, sucking on his cigarlet.

'And now,' said the doctor, 'for the metamorphosis. By a special process,' he explained, 'we are going to show you exactly what happens to this old lady. You are going to witness something never seen before and which may never be seen again!'

The background music rose as the old woman was led into a compartment, faded as the door closed. Colours swirled hypnotically. The calm voice of the doctor returned.

'To understand the process you must realize that the science of the Kaltich is far above that of our own. They have managed to isolate and synthesize the basic elements of life itself. The old woman is now being checked by a machine which is taking over a million readings of her body and comparing them with the minute 'blueprint' which is inherent in every cell. It is finding out just how far she has strayed from the optimum and deciding the exact therapy to rectify the situation. While this is being done we shall play you the famous second movement of Hashman's Subsea Symphony.'

'Bunk,' said Preston. His cigarlet had gone out and he relit it with a shaking hand. 'Bunk,' he repeated. 'A stinking load of rotten fish.'

'How come?' said Ed.

'The whole thing's a phony. That was never the inside of a Gate. You think the Kaltich would ever allow it? And that machine — a prop if ever I saw one.'

'But the treatment's real,' protested Ed. 'What the doc said was basically true.'

'Yes,' Preston admitted. 'It was.' He winced as the music reached a crescendo and turned down the volume. 'Damned racket,' he muttered. 'Why don't they play something from the old days? You don't get music like they used to have,' he complained. 'That smooth beat, that swing . . . ' He shook his head. 'Nothing like it now.'

'You can say that again,' said Ed. He cleared his throat. 'Say, Bill, do you think the pot would stand a little more water?'

'You know where the tap is,' said Preston. He turned up the sound as the music died away. 'Get set for the payoff,' he warned. 'It should be along pretty soon now.'

The music ended; the smiling face of the doctor returned. 'Now,' he said. 'The machine has finished its measurements and the therapy has been determined. To understand what follows you must realize that certain chemical actions take place immediately. The old woman is also under subjective time — that is, a week to her is a minute to us. But why should we worry about details? See now a modern miracle!'

Music, soft, compelling. A swirl of

colour spiraling to a central focal point. Mists of blue, red and green thinned, dissolved. A crone, bent, horrible, stood in the centre of an eye-guiding mesh of lines. Vapour coiled about her feet. Slowly she raised her head. Parchment tight over a living skull, eyes black holes in yellowed bone, lips like an old wound.

Ed made a soft mewing sound.

The crone changed! As they watched the face filled, smoothed, eyes shone where holes had been. The body lifted, swelled, threw back proud shoulders. Hair flowed from the skull, the lips blossomed, the cheeks softened into curves of tender promise.

Cherry Lee, young, radiant, naked and womanhood personified, smiled with heart-twisting triumph.

'And all this,' murmured a persuasive voice, 'can be yours for a mere two thousand galactic units. This new, wonderful exhilarating rejuvenation for as little as a unit a week. Start young and save yourself happiness. From midnight tonight the treatment will be available to all.'

The screen died. Shaking, Preston stared at his friend. Ed coughed, refusing to meet his eyes.

'Did you get it?' demanded Preston savagely. 'Did it register?'

'Two thousand,' muttered Ed. He looked broken, forlorn. 'Two thousand,' he said again. 'Man, I can't even raise one.'

'The payoff,' said Preston. He rose, began to pace the floor of the tiny apartment. Three short steps, turn, three short steps, turn. He swore as he cannoned into the sink-unit, slamming it back into its niche in the wall. 'Two thousand,' he said. 'Double!'

'What you going to do?' asked Ed. He stared at the percolator, forgetting his previous need for more coffee.

'I don't know.' Preston clenched his hands, thinking. Martin had told him not to worry, that his money was safe, and Martin wouldn't lie. But two thousand instead of one? He was over sixty, still healthy but how long would that last? If Martin was only here, could give him that thousand now so he could get it before midnight . . .

'Where're you going?' said Ed.

'Come on.' Preston jerked on his coat. 'I've got to save Martin what I can,' he explained. 'The cash is safe, I know that, but I can't get it without his say-so.' But, he thought, Martin has a partner. He knows me. If I sign a note he'll let me have it for sure. 'Come on,' he said again. 'Hurry!'

5

Charles Denbow gave a final loving polish to the Borgia ring and replaced it carefully in its nest of scarlet velvet. Satisfied, he looked around his shop. The late afternoon sun was just hitting the window and he wondered whether or not to draw the blind. He decided against it. The fading power of the sun would be restricted to the brief time of less than an hour but it was just when the street was at its busiest and customers most probable. He compromised by taking the Japanese prints and the Chinese embroideries from the window, replacing them with a Spanish shawl and a half-dozen items of lesser worth. The prints and embroideries he scattered over a showcase as if he had just been displaying them for a customer's appreciation. Front, he thought. In this business it's all-important. It's not what you sell but how you sell it. The personal touch, he told himself, is as important as the antique.

He turned as the bell jangled over the door. It had a harsh sound, deliberately so, and served as a conversation piece to break the ice. Now, as he moved forward, smiling, ready to make a mild jest, he felt his pulse quicken. It wasn't every day he served the Kaltich. In fact this would be the first time. If he played it right he could be on a bonanza.

'Sire, lady.' He bowed, wondering how to address the two other, younger aliens. Desperate to create a good impression, he took a chance. 'Your graces. My shop is honoured by your presence.'

'He's funny!' The young girl, pretty in her jacket and skirt of brilliant blue, looked at an older version of herself.

'It is impolite to laugh at inferior races,' said her mother sharply. 'You were warned about that.'

'No offence, my lady,' said Denbow quickly. If they should leave now . . . He closed the door firmly behind them, locking it against intrusion. They wore blue and so were only deltas but they were Kaltich and had money. 'Please

66

make yourselves at home,' he invited. 'Would you care for refreshments? Coffee? Tea? Alcohol, perhaps?' For a moment he feared that he had gone too far, been too presumptuous. Then the man grunted.

'We want something special,' he said. 'Something unique to this world. As a memento,' he explained. 'What can you show us?'

'Many things.' Denbow took a deep breath to regain his composure. He might never get a chance like this again. He must not spoil it. 'Something personal? Ornamental? Useful? Rings,' he suggested. 'I have here several from the Borgia collection. They were noted poisoners,' he added. 'Their rings were constructed to contain lethal powders.' He picked one up, demonstrated, held it so as to catch the light. 'Rare,' he said. 'And valuable.'

'We saw better than that on 2204,' said the boy.

'And 5207,' added the girl.

Denbow saw the lack of interest in the eyes of the adults. Hastily he put down the ring and snatched up the Chinese embroidery.

'729,' said the boy.

'That's right,' said his sister. 'Their work makes that thing look like a dirty rag.'

He dropped the embroidery and snatched up a small bust.

'This is seven thousand years old,' he lied. 'A bust of Helen of Troy. The history behind it is unique. It was made from a solid block of alabaster by one of her admirers. He used no tools, having vowed to the gods that he would not sully the stone with dead instruments. Instead he used his fingernails and, probably, his teeth.'

'Why?' The woman was casual.

'Why did he do it, my lady? For love. He thought that his efforts would soften her heart. They didn't,' he added. 'His labour was in vain.'

'How do you know?' said the boy.

'We have our methods,' said Denbow quickly. He hastened to firmer ground. 'Something unique,' he mused, desperately racking his brains. What? What could he show them that they hadn't seen on some other world? Desperate, he took a gamble. After all, they *looked* human. 'I believe I have the very thing,' he said, and hesitated. 'A word in your ear, sire?'

'What is it?' Denbow whispered. The man laughed. 'Why not? Bring it out.'

Fifty minutes later after tea, scotch and biscuits for the children the Kaltich left leaving Denbow a richer and much happier man.

By God, he thought, who would have believed it? A chastity belt of all things. It just goes to show, he told himself. A good salesman can sell anything. But it showed more than that. Who the hell, he thought pleasantly, would have guessed they were so human?

★　★　★

Dipping his brush in the yellow paint, Milt Concord drew a thin line on the curve of the helmet then stepped back to admire his work. That's it, he thought. That does it. Before him the crash helmet, bulky with its attached visor, gay with plumes, shone with new paint. Black and yellow with the big red cross in a circle of white right at the front. Milt belonged to the Medical Messengers and was proud both of his efficiency and his equipment.

Behind a desk in the lobby Miss Watson looked at him with indulgent eyes. It was great to be young, she thought. To be eighteen and doing a good, worthwhile job. Milt wasn't like others of his generation. He didn't belong to a zany group. He was a decent, hard-working boy and if he liked bright colours and a touch of the flamboyant, where was the harm?

'All right if I go for coffee, Miss Watson?' Milt was always polite.

She began to nod, halting the gesture as a light shone on her panel. She stabbed a button. 'Messenger service.'

'I need a new heart,' Hilda Thorenson's voice came clearly over the wire. 'Type 382795193HM. Got that?'

'Just a minute.' Miss Watson picked up her pen and gestured to Milt. 'Wait a minute,' she hissed and then, into the phone, 'What was that number again?'

She wrote it down, pen busy as she

filled in the docket, mouth pursed so as to make no mistake. Carefully she read back the number, waited for the O.K., then hung up the phone. 'Emergency,' she said to Milt. 'Miss Thorenson needs a new heart and fast. The ones in stock are the wrong type.' She stripped the docket from her pad.

Grabbing it, Milt ran from the room. His motorcycle stood outside within the hospital compound. It roared to life at the first kick and he opened the throttle as he headed towards the gate. Only after he'd left the compound did he realize that he'd forgotten his helmet. Darn it, he thought, but perhaps it was all for the best. The paint was still wet. As long as he kept clear of zanies he would be all right.

He opened the throttle, leaning over as he rounded a corner, revelling in the speed, the sound, the pressure of air against his face. Siren wailing, he raced past cars, trucks, intersections and crossings. A police car heard the siren and escorted him for a couple of miles, waving him on as they turned from the route. He braked as an officer, military not police, waved him down.

'This area's closed to traffic,' he said irritably. 'You'll have to take the diversion.'

'Not me,' said Milt importantly. He gestured towards his head, remembered his missing helmet, jerked a thumb over his shoulder to where his badge was painted on the back of his jacket. 'Urgent official business,' he explained. 'Some guy's dying for want of a heart. I'm getting him one.'

'From the Gate?'

'Where else?' Impatiently he revved his engine. 'How about letting me get on with the job?'

'Well, I don't know.' The officer scowled. 'It's murder up there,' he explained. 'Every old guy and his dog are jamming the streets. They all want to get in before the deadline,' he explained. 'You sure you've got to go to the Gate?'

'I'm sure.' Inwardly Milt seethed. What's the matter with the dumb cluck? he thought. Can't he recognize what I am? Hell, if it was him lying back there waiting for a new pump he wouldn't be so obstructive. That's a good word, he told himself. Obstructive. He decided to try it. 'Look,' he said. 'I'm doing a job of work. You don't have to be so obstructive.'

'What's that?' The officer blinked.

'Obstructive,' said Milt. He squeezed the clutch, kicked in the the gear, revved up the engine. Releasing the clutch, he shot away with a roar from his unsilenced exhaust. Almost at once he had to brake. Fuming, jocking his controls, he wove through the crowd. Half a mile and he was there. The perimeter guard checked his docket and jerked his head.

'O.K., inside.'

Milt looked at the crowd bunched up at the perimeter, the sweating policemen forcing them into line, the long queue reaching to the Gate. 'You'll watch the bike?'

'I'll watch it. Now move.'

Milt always felt a little odd walking into a Gate. You've nothing to be afraid of, he told himself. They won't eat you, kidnap you, hold you back. But still he couldn't get over the feeling that now he was on alien territory. They could do anything they liked to him and no one could do anything about it. He'd left the U.S.A. and now . . . somewhere else. Still on Earth, still in the city of New York, but technically on ground which belonged to the Kaltich. Alien soil.

He approached the building, walked around it to the right place, pushed open a door and handed the docket to the man inside. He was completely dressed in white. He took the docket without speaking and turned from the hatch. Milt sat down on a bench against the wall. As always he stared around and with the same result. Just a bare room with a bench and the hatch through which the man had stared. Nothing else. Boldly he stood up and approached the hatch. He could see a small room, a desk with an intercom, a chair and a second hatch on the far side. The man stood before it. As Milt watched he turned and headed towards him. He wore a thick glove on the hand which carried the package.

'Here.' He dropped it and held out a printed form. 'Sign.'

'Just a minute.' Milt was examining the

box. It was of grey fibre, light but colder than ice. He wiped frost from the label. 'Heart,' he read. 'Human male. Tissue type 382795193.'

'Sign,' said the man.

Milt signed, took up the box, ran back to his bike and opened the compartment on the pillion. Vapour rose from the dry ice with which it was packed. He dropped in the package, slammed shut the compartment and roared away.

He felt good, a little like the knights of old when they did something big for their dames. He'd gone out into the world and won a prize for his lady. The fact that Hilda Thorenson didn't know him from Adam made no difference. He knew her. He was in love with her. He would, if she asked, die for her.

The road cleared and he opened his throttle, climbing up through the gears. The bike would do, had done, more than a hundred miles an hour. In the city it was enough.

Wind pressed against his face, forced grit into his eyes. He blinked, seeing vague shapes ahead as if through water, dancing shapes which grew suddenly huge. He leaned over in an effort to avoid them. He felt the jar, the hard yet soggy shock of impact, the sickening realization that he had lost control, was hurtling through the air. The helmet, he thought. I've got no helmet!

Ed Lever swallowed, feeling sick, feeling shaken and totally helpless. It happens like this, he thought. One minute, second even, everything's all right. The next . . . God, he thought. I'll never forget this as long as I live.

He looked down the road to where the motorcyclist was lying. Brains made a red-grey pool from the shattered skull. Well, that's him finished, thought Ed. They can't give him a new brain. He walked to where William Preston had been flung. He lay face upwards, blind eyes staring. He must be all smashed up inside, thought Ed. He looked around, guiltily. People were coming but were still some distance away. Quickly he slipped a hand into the dead man's pocket. Quickly he put the cash into his own.

'I'll pay Martin back,' he told the dead

man. 'I promise that.'

He walked away, quickly, heading towards the Gate. The money would buy him life. Bill couldn't use it now.

* * *

The Prestdale Debt Collection Agency occupied a tiny room in the heart of a run-down business complex which had no elevators, no central heating and no hot running water. All these things had disappeared during the past sixty years. At times Martin wished that the building had followed the amenities.

Climbing the stairs he pushed open the door and caught his partner in a dubious act.

'What the hell?' Tony Dale, his chair leaning back against the wall, yelled at the intruder. Lucile Jones, a pert brunette, squealed as she jumped from his lap and hastily smoothed down her skirt. 'Martin!' Tony let the front legs of his chair down with a bang. 'I thought you were a client,' he said. 'What are you doing here? You're supposed to be on vacation.'

'I was,' said Martin. 'I got bounced by an alien,' he lied. 'He wanted in and I had to get out.'

'Tough.' Tony rose from his chair. 'That's the worst of those toffee-nosed places,' he said. 'No regard for the natives.' He looked at the secretary. 'How about some coffee, kitten?'

'Never mind,' said Martin.

'It won't take a minute,' promised Lucile.

'Forget it.' Martin looked at his partner. 'What's the matter? No more debts to collect?'

'Sure, but — '

'You won't collect them sitting down,' said Martin dryly. 'No matter what the temptation.'

Tony swallowed then, to change the subject. 'Your old man was in,' he said. 'He didn't know you were back. He wanted a grand. Said that it was money you were holding for him. I got him to sign for it. Did I do right?'

Martin frowned. 'What did he want it for?'

'His treatment. He wanted to beat the

deadline — haven't you heard the news?'
He explained as Martin shook his head.
'It made good sense so I let him have it. I
figured you wouldn't object.'

'I don't,' said Martin. He felt a sudden
warmth for his father. He was thinking of
me, he thought. He was trying to save me
money.

'I'd have thought you'd have known
about it,' said Tony. 'It was on all the
screens.'

Martin hadn't been watching. All
morning he'd been busy. At midday the
rough handling he'd had from the ICPM
had demanded either rest or treatment.
He'd spent the afternoon in a Turkish
bath. 'All right,' he said. 'As I'm back I
may as well get on with the job. We both
may as well,' he said meaningfully. 'Dish
them out, Lucile, and let's get moving.'

Late afternoon found him in a sleazy
quarter of the town with a half-dozen
wasted calls behind him. This would be
his last for the day. Outside a tenement he
paused, checked a slip, examined the
names stuck on peeling paper beside a
row of pushbuttons. He scowled. It was

just his luck that the man he wanted lived on the top floor. Jabbing his thumb against the button, he waited for the lock to click, then commenced his climb.

Clancy was an old man with furtive eyes and a voice which held a built-in whine. He looked at Preston as he stood outside the door and cupped a hand behind his ear. 'Hey?' he said. 'What's that again?'

Preston took a deep breath. 'I'm from the Prestdale Collection Agency,' he yelled. 'You owe money — I've come to collect it.'

'Money?' Clancy screwed up his face. He looked, thought Martin, like a monkey. He smelt like a zoo. 'I've got no money.'

'Too bad.' Preston pushed past the old man and entered the apartment. He kicked the door shut behind him. 'You alone?'

'Hey?'

'Are you — hell, never mind.' The apartment consisted of two rooms. He checked it in five seconds. The old man was alone. 'Look, Pop,' he shouted.

'There's a court order against you for 20.70. You got it, I'll go.'

'How much?'

Irritably Preston showed him the order. He blinked at it with his furtive eyes. 'Hell, son,' he said in an aggrieved whine, 'I ain't got that much. Nowhere near that much.'

'Then I'll take something to sell.' Preston looked around. There was a television set in one corner — too big and heavy if there was anything else. Some pots and pans, worthless. An electric fire; an oil-burning heater rusty and probably useless; a set of cutlery, stained and unused in a shabby leatherette case. Some moldering clothes. A battered clock. 'Hell, Pop,' he said disgustedly. 'Haven't you got anything worth 20.70?'

'No, son. Like a drink?'

'I'd like 20.70,' said Preston. It's another bust, he thought. Another crumb without a minim to his name. Why do shops give these old people credit when they know all the time they won't be able to pay? But then, he told himself, they don't have to do the dirty work. They expect us to do that. 'Look,' he yelled. 'You pay me or I'll take stuff to sell. That,' he said, looking around, 'means I'll take it all. The TV, the fire, the cutlery . . . ' He broke off, thinking. Snatching up a knife he examined it. It was black with tarnish and he doubted if it would have cut butter.

'That's a fish knife,' said Clancy. 'They're all fish knives, forks too. Real silver. I had 'em for a wedding present,' he said, 'forty years ago now.' His eyes grew cunning. 'They're worth a lot,' he said. 'Twice what I owe. You take them and give me the balance in cash.'

An optimist, thought Preston. Well, you can't blame him for trying. He filled out a form and held the pad to the old man. 'I'll take them in settlement of your debt,' he said. 'Is that all right with you?'

'What about the cash difference?'

'No cash. I'll sell them and you can collect anything over by applying to the office within seven days.' He wouldn't of course, none of them ever did. 'If you agree sign and press your thumb on that square.' He tore off the bottom copy and gave it to the old man. Clancy took it.

'Is this all I get?'

'Yes,' said Preston. 'That's all.'

Outside in the street Preston felt the familiar weight of defeat. The knives and forks were probably only worth a score when brand, shining new. He'd be lucky to get a third of that. He'd bought the debt for a quarter-value. Less than two units profit, he thought. How not to get rich fast!

It was close to dusk. He was tired and decided to call it a day. He heard the ring of the phone as he reached his utiliflat, hurrying when he realized that perhaps his father would still be out. The place smelt of coffee, soy bean soup and stale cigarlet smoke. He snatched up the phone, listened, slowly put it down.

Efficient, he thought dully. That's one thing about the municipal authorities you can't complain about. They were damned efficient — especially when it came to demanding the charge for ambulance and crematorial services.

He's dead, he told himself. My father, dead: I'll never see him again. We'll never make plans for the future because now, for him, there is no future. Killed in the street, picked up, cremated immediately because they simply haven't the room to hold a corpse longer than they have to. And they send me the news with the bill.

Suddenly he was sick of it, the whole stinking mess. I'm wasting my life, he thought. The only bit of decent living I've ever known was at the schloss and that didn't last. Damn the Kaltich, he thought with sudden fury. They killed him. Doubling the charges like that. If they hadn't he would still be here, alive, not ashes in a sewer.

He looked down, found the phone book, searched for a number. Impatiently he punched it out.

He heard the click of an answering machine.

'Miss Thorenson is not at home but you may record any message you wish to leave. Miss Thorenson is not at home but — '

'This is Martin Preston,' he said curtly. 'I've changed my mind.'

6

Hilda Thorenson had more than beautiful hands. Nude, she displayed the idealised figure of a Scandinavian statue. She dived and swam with the speed and grace of a porpoise. Three times Preston tried to catch her and each time she left him standing. Finally they left the pool and sat basking in the sun.

'I'm not going to ask you why you changed your mind,' she said. 'That's your business. But this isn't a game and you could get yourself killed. You realise that?'

'I've had three days to think about it,' he said dryly.

'I'm sorry but . . . busy, busy, busy. A surgeon's work is never done.'

Just as well, he thought. Hilda Thorenson lived in the penthouse of an apartment building standing in the most fashionable part of town. It had fifteen rooms, a sauna bath and a private theatre. Outside were a garden, barbecue pit and a swimming pool. Retractable plastic covers protected the exterior from inclement weather. He couldn't begin to guess at the rent but it must have been astronomical. When he said so she shrugged.

'You are ill,' she said. 'You need a new heart and you will die without it. How much is it worth to you?'

He hesitated.

'All you own,' she said. 'What's the good of money when you're dead?'

'So you get well paid,' he said.

'I get very well paid,' she corrected. 'I'm good at my work. I know it and my clients know it. A lot of them are grateful.' She looked at him. 'You're young,' she said. 'Handsome. You have a lot to lose.'

'And quite a bit to gain,' he reminded. 'What are the odds?'

'Of you collecting that two million? Small,' she said honestly. 'You won't be the first to have tried. Some of the best minds of Earth have grappled with the problem. The Kaltich are smart. They've got us in a stranglehold. Have you ever wondered,' she said, 'why the governmental forces haven't just gone in and grabbed a Gate? Just taken it over?'

He nodded.

'They have. Five years after the Kaltich appeared they tried it. In Estonia. The Soviets sent in armed troops. They managed to get what they were after — and found they had nothing at all. The Kaltich had retreated and closed the Gate after them.'

'What happened?'

'For thirty years no member of the Communist Part was granted longevity treatment. The heads of the party were old men. No government has dared try it since. That's why the Kaltich have us in a stranglehold. Your worst enemies are those of your own kind.'

'Are you saying that STAR is against me?'

'No. We are the ones who are for you, but how many belong to STAR? Not many,' she said, not waiting for an answer. 'And we could be wrong. The UNO thinks that we are. Chung Hoo preaches patience — all will come if we wait long enough. I think that he is lying. Not consciously but actually. He doesn't want to recognize the truth.'

'Which is?'

'The Gates will never be opened,' she said. 'Not as they've promised. Not so that the people of Earth can enjoy new worlds. We're trapped,' she said. 'Beaten by our own greed. Tell me,' she demanded. 'Do you know how far science has advanced since the aliens came?'

He shook his head.

'Hardly at all. Oh, we've made some slight progress, perfected some skills, tied up a few loose ends, but that's about all. We haven't made any really significant progress during the past fifty years. Can you guess why?'

It was obvious. 'Why beat your brains out trying to do something that has already been done? All we need to do is to wait and the Kaltich will drop the answer to every question right smack in our lap.'

'Exactly. They've even killed our initiative.'

An inflated rubber duck lay at the edge of the pool. He picked it up and threw it into the water. Idly he watched it drift. The sunshine made rainbows on the tiny puddles where they had dripped water when climbing out.

'Wait,' he said. 'For how long?'

'Until we're so helplessly dependent on the Kaltich that we'll be no better than slaves.' She stretched, breasts high and firm. 'I'm a surgeon,' she said. 'Did you know that spare-part surgery was possible as far back as the middle of last century? The point is that we could have had our own spare-part organic banks by this time. In fact, we did. Then the Kaltich offered to keep us supplied. They taught us their method of tissue-typing. Now, when we need anything, we send to a Gate.' She rolled, looking directly at him. 'Where,' she asked meaningfully, 'do they get those spare parts?'

Moodily he lit a cigarlet. You're avoiding the issue, he thought. STAR has already gone into these questions. She's marking time for some reason of her own. Idly he wondered how a woman like her, rich, beautiful, had come to join the organization.

'I deal with a varied clientele,' she explained. 'One of them spoke to me about STAR, so I joined.

'Just like that?'

'Well, no,' she admitted. 'At first I contributed funds, then advice, then I took a more active part. The love of adventure, I suppose,' she said. 'The thrill of belonging to a secret organization. Surgery can be very boring.' She stretched, the soft flesh of her breasts flattening on the marble edging the pool as she reached for one of his cigarlets. 'And you?'

'I don't really know,' he said broodingly. 'I was bored too, I guess, eager for a little excitement. No,' he admitted. 'It wasn't that. I just don't like the Kaltich. I don't like the way they lord it around. The way they whip people.' Unconsciously his hand lifted to touch his cheek. 'This plan of yours,' he said. 'When are you going to tell me about it?'

'In a minute.' She moved her knee, one long, curved thigh sliding over the inside of the other. Her skin was like velvet, soft, enticing with the promise of tactile pleasure. Tiny blonde hairs shone like a golden down in the bright sunshine. 'We were talking of spare-parts,' she said. 'The aliens can supply them and they can come from only one place — here on Earth. The tissue is too similar for them to have come from anywhere else.'

'The people they let pass through the Gate,' he said. 'The young selectees.'

'It could be. We think so. It makes sense.'

Then why use them? he thought, but knew the answer. To a dying man morals and ethics have little meaning. And, he thought bitterly, what you don't know doesn't hurt.

'They do it for money,' she said. 'Have you ever worked out just how much money they make?'

'Tell me.'

'They charged a thousand units for one longevity treatment. Now it's doubled. Everyone over fifty wants one. They want to look and feel like thirty again. So they pay.' She removed the cigarlet from between her lips and examined the glowing tip. 'We estimate that, from North America alone, they collect ten thousand million units a year. That's just for the longevity treatment. No one knows how much they collect for the sale of spare parts.'

'That's ten million times the average income,' he said thoughtfully. 'And soon to be doubled. What do they do with it?'

'Buy things. They own almost all of New York. They own airlines, farms, factories, power plants. You name it they've got it. And they buy food,' she said. 'Fantastic amounts of food. And guns. And ammunition.'

'Why? Do you think they want to start a war?'

'I don't know.' She threw away the cigarlet. 'I just state the facts. STAR has been collecting data and we don't like what we've found. In another twenty years the Kaltich will practically own the planet. In another fifty we'll all be working for the aliens. Then what?'

'We won't let them get away with it,' he said. 'We daren't.'

'Who is 'we'?' she demanded. 'You? Me? The guy next door? What the hell can we do about it? Nothing,' she said, answering herself. 'The governments are for the aliens and they'll keep us in line.

It's happened before,' she said. 'The old North American Indians were robbed blind, dispossessed of their land, herded into reservations. I guess they thought it could never happen to them either. But it did. You know,' she said, looking at him, 'the more I think about it the more it scares me. We've been invaded and don't know it. We've been taken over without a struggle. Almost without a struggle. Thank God for STAR.'

'Yes,' he said flatly. 'I expect Lassiter felt like that.'

'He was unlucky,' she said. 'But let's face it. What is one man's life in a war to regain a planet?'

'That depends on whose life you're talking about.' Preston crushed out the butt of his cigarlet and threw it at the inflated duck. The filter made a popping sound as it hit the rubber. 'Listen,' he said. 'I've enjoyed the swim and everything else, but I can do without the build-up. Why don't you just tell me about the plan?'

She looked at him, moving so as to let gravity claim her breasts, smiling at the

93

involuntary motion of his eyes. 'Now?'

In the pool the duck bobbed, watching.

★   ★   ★

'Beta,' said Preston. 'Gamma. Delta. Gamma-delta. Delta-alpha.'

'Look again.' Hilda Thorenson pressed the remote control and the slide jumped back onto the screen.

'Delta-alpha-null,' he said. 'I hadn't noticed the black on the badge.'

'Try this one.' A Kaltich, dressed all in black, showed on the screen.

'Null.'

'Now this.'

'Null-alpha,' he said. The man was all in black but this time wore a red flash. A third null appeared, this time with a flash of yellow and blue. 'Null-beta-delta.'

'And this?'

'Delta-null.'

'Delta-null-epsilon,' she corrected. 'You missed the white at the bottom of the flash. Now this . . . and this . . . and this . . . '

It went on for another hour. Finally

Hilda Thorenson pressed the switch and the screen went blank. She wore a figure-hugging robe of scarlet velvet; the thick tresses of her golden hair hung loose about her shoulders. In the dimness of the theatre her skin shone with a limpid translucence. 'That's enough,' she said. 'If you don't know about their badges of rank by now you never will.'

Like coat armour, he thought, remembering the schloss. But no, these badges weren't to identify the wearer in a personal sense.

'To sum up,' she said briskly, 'as far as we know all the Kaltich are divided into six classes; red, yellow, green, blue, white and black. A member of one class shows his superiority over other members of the same class by wearing a badge. A beta with a red flash is of higher rank than a beta with a green. A beta with no badge is lower than both and so on. Whites, the epsilons, seem to be of the lowest civilian rank. Nulls, the blacks, are the military or the law-enforcement body. What,' she demanded, 'does this tell you?'

'A caste system,' he said. 'Something

like the Hindus.'

'Nothing else?'

'Such a system is usually unadaptable. A member of one class cannot, or will not, perform the duties of another.'

'And?'

'It is brittle,' he said slowly, thinking. 'Inflexible.'

'It is also concerned, to a remarkable degree, with symbols of status and position. Think of the army,' she suggested. 'Any army. There you have an almost exact analogy. Privates, noncommissioned officers, officers . . . a multiple layer of various degrees of command. Now, if a private were to adopt the uniform of an officer — who would expose the impersonation? The men?'

'I doubt it. They wouldn't risk being wrong.'

'Exactly. Their own system works to protect the impersonator.' Her eyes shone in the shadowed dimness. 'That,' she said quietly, 'is the plan.'

Before he could answer she operated the remote control and the screen blazed with colour. This time it was a movie. A family of Kaltich dressed all in blue were shown wandering down a street.

'Look at them,' she ordered. 'A man, a woman, two children. An ordinary family. Tourists.'

'So?'

'We're getting a lot more of them,' she said. 'Groups like this one, family groups, travelling, looking around, staying at local hotels. The Kaltich, it seems, have lifted some form of restriction. Those people are vacationing.' The movie blurred, slowed to show a couple of men dressed in green. 'Gamma out sightseeing. They eat, drink and act like ordinary people. Exactly like ordinary people. If we took one and dressed him in our clothing you wouldn't be able to tell him from a native.'

'So you imagine that, if one of us should dress like one of them, the converse would apply?' Preston frowned, thinking about it. 'Would it be as simple as that? Surely they must have some form of identification?'

'They probably have,' she agreed. 'But I'm not just talking about dressing up like one of the Kaltich. It goes deeper than that. Listen,' she said. 'You were sent for because of three things: you speak perfect Galactic, you are loyal to STAR — and you look almost exactly like a delta we've got on ice. That's right,' she said. 'I told you they acted just as if they were human. This one was lured away from his friends. He was on vacation and we made sure that he enjoyed it. We've got some attractive girls working for STAR,' she added. 'He fell for one like a ton of bricks.'

'And?'

'She took him to a hotel. He was doped and we went over him with a fine-tooth comb. Controlled hypnosis — we dragged out all we could find. You're going to assimilate all we learned. You've got two days. In that time you're going to stop being human and become a Kaltich.'

He took out his cigarlets, lit one for himself, another for the woman. Smoke drifted before the glowing screen.

'The Gate,' he said. 'Maybe they have a encephalogram-check, something like that. The Kaltich aren't fools. In the past fifty years others must have tried this.'

'Maybe they have, we don't know. STAR hasn't.' She drew smoke into her lungs, blew it out in a spreading cloud. 'You've got a good point,' she admitted, 'but we've covered it. This delta comes from the Washington Gate. We lured him to New York and made sure that his friends knew about it. Now suppose we had a vicious riot. One bad enough to shatter the ring of perimeter guards. And assume that in the middle of all the fuss and excitement a group of Kaltich should come running towards the Gate. They would be chased, apparently in danger of their lives. Would the Gate custodian be so insistent on identification then? And, even if they were, could they check with Washington before letting you pass into safety?'

'Maybe not,' he admitted, and then, 'so this is the wonderful plan.'

'It'll work,' she said. 'Do you think STAR's been idle all this time? Those fires and demonstrations aren't spontaneous. STAR is behind most of the zanies. And this is our big chance. The doubling of the longevity charge,' she explained.

'There have been demonstrations each night since then. When we're ready there'll be a big one. In the chaos you'll get your chance to walk into the Gate. You won't be alone. You'll be with others. If you're smart you'll let them carry you.'

'So I get into the Gate,' he said. 'What then?'

She shrugged. 'I don't know. That's up to you. We can't do more than give you your chance.'

'And the man I'm to impersonate?'

'Forget him,' she said. 'He won't bother you. This is war, remember? What is one life against the destiny of the world?'

On the screen the aliens still walked and talked and acted like ordinary humans. He reached out, took the switch from her hand and pressed it. In the following dimness he touched her knee, slid his hand along her thigh. 'You're beautiful,' he said in English. 'So very beautiful.'

'Fool!' She had muscles and used them. The impact of her hand numbed the side of his face. 'Never use other than

100

Galactic! Never!'

He rubbed his cheek, watching her.

'But thank you' she said softly. 'Thank you very much.'

She wore nothing beneath the robe.

7

All Celestial Gates followed the same pattern; a central dome flanked by long, low structures a little like flattened aircraft hangars, each standing in the centre of an expanse of open ground. Only the extent of the ground varied — the Gate in Moscow sat in ten acres, in London a quarter. The New York Gate was even more modest and Preston was glad of it.

He ran towards the building with four others all wearing the vivid blue of the deltas. Like clowns, he thought with a strange detachment, or men in fancy dress — but, he reminded himself, this is no party you're going to. This is serious. He thought of Lassiter and his severed hands. What, he wondered, would happen to him should his disguise be penetrated?

Unconsciously he slowed, falling back from the others towards the crowd following close behind. The perimeter guards were lost in the organized chaos. A strategic fire blazed to one side, a leaping column of dancing colours. Overhead helicopters whirled their belly-floods showering swathes of light. The voice of the mob was a hungry roar.

STAR, thought Preston, had done a good job. Good for him, if for no one else. Certainly not good for the old people who had been attracted to the Gate by lying propaganda, nor for those who must have been injured or killed. Did it always take the magic of blood, he wondered, to ensure the success of a plan?

He stumbled and almost fell. The delta just ahead of him turned, his face ashen. 'Keep up, man,' he rapped. 'Those people are animals.'

The man wore a flash of red which made him Preston's superior. He was glad of it. His own badge of yellow put him above the other three but the other man would give the orders. In a situation like this it was always easier to follow than to lead.

He stumbled again as they reached the

building. The side doors were sealed, only the central opening with its ramp and unloading bays gave access to the Gate. A cluster of men in white, epsilons, worked stolidly at a pile of crates. Before them stood a null. He carried a squat-barrelled weapon and made an urgent gesture.

'This way, sirs. Hurry!'

Other nulls, similarly armed, appeared behind the first. Deploying, they dropped to one knee and aimed their weapons. From the rear of the crowd a magnesium flare climbed into the sky to hang a man-made star.

'Hold your fire!' The delta-alpha stared at the crowd. The front ranks were slowing, veering to either side, turning back so as to avoid the menace of the nulls.

'Shoot them!' One of the others, a delta-gamma, glared at the milling mass outside the opening. 'They would have killed us,' he said. 'Torn us to pieces. Kill them like the animals they are!'

'Hold your tongue, Egart!'

'Yes, sir, but — '

'They're going,' said the delta-alpha.

And then, to the null, 'Is everyone inside?'

'Yes, sir.'

'Seal the Gate.' A slab of reinforced concrete fell from the roof and sealed the opening. 'All right,' said the officer. 'Report for interrogation.'

Preston followed the others calmly. His brain seemed to be alight with odd, seemingly unrelated scraps of information. Those epsilons, for example. They were loading crates onto a conveyor belt. The belt would carry them through the Gate but, before they reached it, they would pass through an electronic death trap which would take care of any bug, insect, vermin or unwanted stranger. There would be no risk of tarantulas among the bananas, no snakes among the fruit. No insidious germ. And no men. Nothing living could resist the barrier.

Write off one method of crashing the Gates.

Preston kept moving, following the rest, knowing where they were going and gaining confidence from the knowledge. Gamma Eldon was at his desk as they entered his office. He leaned back, looking at the first man. 'Well?'

'We were on vacation, sir. There was trouble, a riot of some kind, and we were advised to stay in our hotel.'

'Advised? By whom?'

'UNO men, sir,' he said, and Preston felt a perverse satisfaction. The men had been operatives of STAR but UNO would get the credit — as they would have got the blame.

'I see. Continue.'

'After a while we were advised to make a run for the Gate. We did so.' He turned and gestured to Preston. 'He joined us on the way.'

Eldon nodded. 'Very good. Go and report in.' He lifted a hand as Preston made to follow the others. 'Not you. Name?'

'Leon Tonoch, sir. I'm from the Washington Gate,' he said quickly. 'My details will not be on record here.'

'Why did you return to this Gate?'

'I've been very foolish, sir,' said Preston. He produced identifying papers from his pocket. The whip dangling from his wrist made a tapping sound on the

106

edge of the desk as he laid them before the gamma. 'As you see, I was on vacation. I parted from the rest of my party. There was a girl,' he explained. 'I found her attractive. We travelled to New York together. I joined the others because I thought it best.'

The truth, he thought, the first rule of any successful agent. Never lie if it can be avoided. But, he told himself, you don't have to tell all of the truth. Would the real Tonach? The thought was dangerous. He *was* Tonach. His life depended on him remembering that.

Eldon looked at the papers and picked up a phone. It was almost exactly like any Earth instrument. 'Get me the Washington Gate,' he said, and then to Preston. 'Stand over there. On that black circle. Do not move.' He spoke into the phone. 'Keyman? Eldon here. Do you have a Leon Tonach, delta-beta attached to you? Yes, I'll wait.' Idly he examined the papers Preston had given him. 'Yes. That's right,' he said into the phone. 'Yes. Very good, Gamma Keyman. I'll attend to it immediately.'

He replaced the handset and stared at Preston. 'You,' he said curtly, 'are under arrest.'

★ ★ ★

The punishment was seven lashes of a major whip. Preston took them on his naked back, ceremoniously, watched by every delta attached to the New York Gate. A null delivered the punishment. He didn't need to use much force. The barbs were sharp; the nerve-poison did the rest.

Preston lost consciousness at the second lash. He lost it again when they cut him down. He woke and screamed his throat raw before kindly blackness engulfed him for a third time. It didn't last. He was dimly conscious of movement but all else was hidden by a red veil of pain. He became aware that he was in a cell eight feet square with a barred door, a single light, a cot and nothing else. The cot was of canvas stretched taut over a metal frame. Whimpering, he rolled over onto his face, blood running from bitten lips. The nails of his fingers dug crescent wounds into his palms.

From time to time a null brought water, watching incuriously as he fumbled it into his mouth. Finally he was able to speak.

'Where am I?'

'Washington Gate, sir.'

The use of a title was informative and so was his location. A race who moved between the stars would think nothing of transferring him to another city. The null had been respectful. Perhaps there was yet hope.

Food came with the water and, after a long time, a clean uniform. Then, when the pain had eased, the door swung open and he was free. Free of the cell if nothing else.

'The punishment was severe but you deserved it.' Gamma Keyman looked thoughtfully at Preston as he stood in his office. It was a twin to that used by Eldon. Even the black circle on the floor was in the same position. Preston stood on it knowing that a touch on a button and he would be dead. The Kaltich took no chances. 'Do you agree that the punishment was merited?'

'Yes, sir.' To have argued would have been useless. Had Hilda Thorenson known what he was getting into? She tapped Tonach's mind, thought Preston. Surely she must have known. Or perhaps she hadn't bothered to find out. Or, he thought, perhaps she hadn't told him for obvious reasons. No sane man would willingly suffer such agony.

'Aside from the fact that you deliberately left your party, that you fraternized with a local woman and that you travelled beyond your permitted area, you chose to return to the New York Gate. Four violations, three serious, one both unnecessary and undesirable.' Gamma Keyman leaned back in his chair. 'It did not please me to have the transgressions of one of my subordinates known to others.'

'My apologies, sir,' said Preston humbly. He was beginning to understand. The Kaltich were human in their rivalries. 'I lost my head,' he confessed. 'I didn't think of what I was doing. I deeply regret any inconvenience I may have caused. My punishment was more than just.' His voice was husky, strained from his recent ordeal.

Mollified, the gamma allowed himself to relax. 'All right, Tonach. I understand. These local women ... ' He made an expressive gesture, 'But rules are not made to be broken.'

'I realise that, sir.'

'You seem to have the correct attitude and that is to your credit,' mused Keyman. 'I don't think this need go any further.'

'Thank you, sir. I appreciate that.' Pile it on, thought Preston savagely. Be humble, eat dirt, but keep him happy.

'I'm returning you to duty,' the gamma decided. 'Your back will be sore for a while, but that can't be helped. You will also have to work an extra turn to make up for the time you were incommoded. I imagine,' he said dryly, 'that it seemed a long ten days.'

It had seemed an eternity. 'Very long, sir,' said Preston. 'I can assure you sir, that it will never happen again.' Not, he mentally added, if I have to kill every last dammed one of you.

'That's the spirit,' said Keyman. 'Now report for duty.'

His luck held. Those who had been close to the original Tonach, the ones he had worked with and with whom he had gone on vacation, were no longer at the Gate. They had been moved elsewhere. Or perhaps, he thought, it wasn't luck at all. Perhaps it had been a part of the plan. So far STAR had managed things well. Aside from the beating, of course. He could never forgive them for that.

The duty was simple and left plenty of time for thought. He had to check deliveries against manifests, a thing any bright moron could have done without difficulty, certainly the epsilon-alpha who was in charge of the unloading crews. It's the system, he thought. Caste dictates who should do what. They unload, handle the crates, do the heavy work. I oversee. And investigate. That's why I'm here. Well, he told himself, get on with it. You're in. So far you've been accepted and are safe. Now make the Kaltich pay for what they've done.

And he reminded himself, earn two million units for doing it.

*   *   *

Gammas didn't run the Gate. There were four of them working in six-hour turns of duty. Above them were two betas and somewhere was an alpha in supreme charge. The epsilons were the labour force; they carried no whips. The nulls did the dirty work. They were the wardens, the guards, the military police. Like the epsilons they carried no whips but bore arms instead.

So much STAR had verified from Tonach and what they had learned Preston knew. It wasn't enough. I'm like a noncommissioned officer, he thought. I can move around and I know enough of the system to play the part, but that's about all. The real secret, the important thing, I don't know. Would an ordinary NCO have known about the workings of a military computor? As yet he hadn't seen the Gate and, apparently, neither had Tonach. And that didn't make sense.

113

The man had travelled through it; he must have known that at least. He had known it, Preston decided. Known it and, somehow, been prevented from relaying the information. Hypnosis, he thought. A fine tool — if you know exactly what questions to ask and how to ask them.

Irritably he slammed the door of his room. It was a comfortable room, the furnishings luxurious, the little, personal things showing a regard for fine quality. A record player and a stack of records. A projector and a heap of film. A fine camera. A collection of expensive liqueurs, some familiar, others not. A peculiar device with a helmet-like attachment and a studded keyboard. A transparent jar in which drifted slowly twisting strands of living crystal, growing, changing, a mobile kaleidoscope of shimmering colour. A three-dimensional photograph of a smiling, beautiful woman.

He picked it up and soft words whispered from the image.

'Leon, darling, I love you so much. All the time I think of you so far away from me. It is your duty, I know, darling, and it will soon be over. But it seems so long *to wait before we are together for always. I was at the emigration bureau the other day and they have such a wonderful selection of places. When you are home we must go down and register for one. Our own house, darling, with land and workers and everything. Oh, my dearest, when we are together I shall . . . '*

The voice grew softer, more intimate. Preston put down the photograph. The Kaltich women, at least, were far from inhibited. He wondered if she would sorrow too much at never again seeing her man.

Damn them, he thought. Among themselves they're human enough — why can't they be the same outside? He knew the answer. The colonial complex. Others were inferiors, savages, slaves. Only the Kaltich could be thought of as equals.

He picked up the helmet and slipped it on his head. Nothing. He punched buttons and, suddenly, the room was a swirling mass of colour. He punched more and a thin, high-pitched singing echoed in his ears. More and, with shocking abruptness, he was a terrified

115

animal caught in hampering strands of sticky mesh. At the corner of his vision something horrible slowly advanced.

Preston ripped off the helmet and stood shaking. Mental recordings, he thought. The agony of a creature trapped, terrified, knowing what was to come. For amusement, he told himself. Titivation to pass time. How decadent could you get?

And how rich? The room reeked of money spent with a careless disregard. Nothing but the best, he noted. For the Kaltich, nothing but the best. The best from Earth and how many other worlds?

The helmet was alien. The jar of growing crystal. The photograph betrayed a technology higher than he knew. But he could learn nothing of use in this place. Toys, items to amuse, things to beguile the time. And he dared not waste time.

Impatiently he left the room, passed down a passage, entered the door of a recreation room. Men, deltas, sat at tables playing games of chance. One waved at him.

'Care to sit in, Leon?'

'No thanks.'

'Come on. You owe me a chance to get revenge.'

Preston shook his head. The man knew him, only casually perhaps, but it was enough. There could be references to past activities, the mention of common acquaintances, a hundred little things including the game he did not know how to play.

'What's the matter? Don't you want to know me now?'

'Leave him alone.' Another player leaned over and said something in a low voice.

The first man shrugged. 'All right. I didn't know. But how long's it going to be before he gets over it?' And then, to Preston, 'Sorry, Leon. Some other time, uh?'

Outside he paused, thinking. The Gate itself must lie in the centre of the complex; that seemed the most logical place for it to be. The living accommodation and offices must be built around it, both for protection and for quick access. That meant a passage must lead to where he wanted to go. He began to search for it, using both Tonach's information and his own instinct. Both let him down. He found a promising door but it was firmly locked. The alternative was obvious.

Quickly he retraced his steps back to the central opening, the ramp and unloading bays. The conveyor belt must lead directly to the Gate. He followed it until it ran into a tunnel. Back again he looked thoughtfully at the ramp. Trucks, he thought, could be driven along it. It was obvious that those same trucks must go somewhere and, if it was ever decided to move heavy equipment, it would have to travel by truck. The reasoning was excellent — but the ramp was sealed further in by heavy doors.

And to go by the tunnel was to pass through the death trap.

★ ★ ★

There was only one thing left to do.

The null was easy, relaxed, standing a routine honour guard. He looked at Preston as he approached, automatically stiffening into a position of respect. 'Sir?'

'Medical.'

'A moment, sir. Your name, please?' Preston told him, waiting as the man did things with a wall-communicator. 'Very good, sir. You may pass.'

Tight, thought Preston as he walked past the guard. They don't like the lesser ranks walking about in certain areas. The epsilons, he knew, were housed in subterranean apartments. The nulls had their own barracks. Only the higher command, apparently, had direct access to the Gate.

They made a mistake, he thought. STAR didn't think this thing through far enough. I should have taken the place of a gamma at least. But no, he told himself. That wouldn't have worked either. There aren't enough of them. Or perhaps they couldn't find one who looked enough like me. He was speculating, a waste of time. Now he needed all his concentration.

The medical room was ahead. He had to enter it. He was expected and to fail to show up would be to start an alarm. The doctor was a gamma-alpha. He looked at Preston as an assistant took down details.

'The trouble, sir?'

'My back.' It was a genuine excuse. 'It's hurting and I wondered — '

'You are the man who was punished?' The doctor was curt.

Preston nodded. 'That's right, sir. Leon Tonach.'

'You must know that the after-effects of the whipping are an integral part of your discipline. I shall report you for having wasted our time.'

'Yes, sir.' Well, thought Preston, that was soon over. He turned left as he left the medical room, walking in the opposite direction to which he had came. Quickly he ran downstairs, along a passage, pushed open a door. It led to another a few feet away. He opened it and stared at the Gate.

It could be nothing else.

But it was like nothing he had expected.

It was a double arch, rounded, fifteen feet from stem to stem and twenty high. A gigantic letter *m*. One half of it was blank, the entire arch filled with nothing but a dead, flat black surface which hurt his eyes as he looked at it. The other was clear, aside from a peculiar shivering as of air disturbed by rising currents of heat. He looked through it and saw the ramp, the walls leading to the central opening. The tilt of the ramp prevented him from seeing outside. Penetrating it in an unbroken line, the length of the conveyor-belt tunnel marred the symmetry of the arch.

A man walked through the black surface.

He came as if walking through mist, stepping from the arch as a man would step from one room into another, casual, doing a thing to which he was long accustomed. He wore red, an alpha. He halted as he saw Preston.

'You! What are you doing here?'

Preston bowed, gesturing towards the door through which he had come.

'I asked you a question!' The alpha let his hand fall to his whip. The lash made a thin, vicious sound as it cut through the air. 'Answer me!'

'I was about to pass through the Gate, sir.'

'Alone?' The man glanced at the other arch. 'There is something wrong,' he decided. 'You will turn and walk before me.' The whip almost touched Preston's cheek. 'Move!'

Preston hit him in the stomach.

The man was soft, flabby; his stomach felt like dough. He doubled, gasping and Preston slammed the stiffened edge of his palm hard against the nape of his neck. The alpha fell, turning a little so that the outflung whip fell against the blackness of the arch.

Preston ripped at his clothes.

Camouflage, he thought. I've got to take the chance. A delta's nothing in this setup. I need more weight, more authority. Luck, he told himself. You've had the luck of the devil so far. Let's hope that it lasts just a little longer. Long enough for me to change clothes with this character and get away from here.

The red uniform was a little too large but the belt took up most of the slack. He picked up the man's whip then paused, looking at it. The tip had been severed as though with a knife, the metal bright and perfectly flat. He frowned at it, then at the blackness of the arch. Cautiously he reached out with the whip and touched the surface. He felt a slight resistance and pressed harder. The metal of the whip dissolved as he watched. He shoved and looked at the stump in his hand. At his feet the dead man stared at him as if guessing what was in his mind.

Thirty seconds later Preston stepped boldly through the clear archway. He felt a momentary tingle and that was all. Turning, he saw blackness, while now the other arch was clear. He swallowed, forcing himself to look, but didn't see what he'd expected. No limp body in delta blue. No head and upper torso, hands and shoulder in red and vanished ruin.

He shook his head, impatient with himself. This was war. The alpha had been an enemy and had died as Lassiter had died. The fact that he couldn't be seen was something to worry about in the future. Now he had to make good his escape.

He walked from the Gate, past bowing

nulls, past working epsilons, striding from the building and out into the clean, unsullied air.

Unsullied because there was no mass of sprawling buildings, no snarling traffic, no stench of fumes and dirt and too many people in too small a space. Instead there were slender pyramidical structures, tall and graceful in the bright sunshine. The green of grass and trees, the bright touches of colour from massed flowers.

By God, he thought with rising excitement. I've done it. I've really done it. I'm the first Earthman to set foot on another world!

8

A low musical note sounded from behind. Preston turned. A hover-truck, the rear stacked high with crates, came sighing down the ramp. It slowed as it drew level as if the driver expected a signal then, as Preston continued walking, it passed him to vanish behind some trees. Ten minutes later, when he was wishing he'd flagged a lift, he came to the first of the pyramidical structures.

They were tents, a whole village of tepees, tall, sheeted plastic drawn over thin aluminium tubes and daubed with primitive designs of glaring colour. The people he saw grouped about the tents or walking the unpaved ground between had a strange familiarity. Zanies, he thought, then corrected himself. Not zanies but those the kids tried to emulate. Indians. Red Indians from the old North American west.

Slowly he walked through the village.

There was an absence of smells generally associated with such a place. The few dogs were well-fed and well-behaved. The children were restrained. He halted beside a man and examined his equipment. The bow was of steel, the arrows feathered with nylon. The knife and hatchet were of polished metal. The clothes, fringed and painted, had the appearance of synthetic fibre. He looked into a tent. A woman, wide-eyed, held back a small child. The floor was covered with rugs and blankets. Pieces of equipment hung from the walls.

Preston looked at the man. 'What world is this?'

'Sire?' The Galactic was thick guttural, but perfectly understandable.

'This world — what is its name?'

'Sire, forgive me, but I do not understand.'

Dumb, thought Preston. He looked at the stolid brown face, the dull eyes. Unconsciously his hand fell to the whip dangling from his wrist. His own whip — that belonging to the alpha had been destroyed. The man cringed.

'Forget it,' said Preston, and walked on through the village.

The tents were clustered to either side, leaving a broad central avenue. Midway along stood a group of solid buildings made of unpeeled logs. One looked as if it might be a grain store. Another was obviously a blacksmith's. A third looked like a livery stable. Facing it was a long, low cabin with unwindowed extensions at the rear. A hitching rail faced it and a water trough stood to one side. The place had a wide veranda on which stood tables and chairs. It was an uneasy blend of an old western trading post and a French sidewalk cafe. Kaltich were at the tables, eating, drinking or just sitting engaged in conversation. Native women moved between them carrying drinks and plates of food. The sight woke Preston's hunger.

He climbed on the veranda, sat at a table, gestured to a waitress. 'Food,' he demanded. 'And something to drink.'

'Yes, sire.' The girl was pretty in a swarthy kind of way. She wore a fringed garment, belted around her waist, coming to just above the knee. A rope of cut-glass beads hung around her neck. 'We have steak, sire. Would that be satisfactory?'

Preston nodded.

'And wine, sire? Or would you prefer tiswin?'

'Wine,' decided Preston. 'Red. And something to smoke,' he added. 'Cigarlets. Number one size.' What the hell, he thought, let's make the most of this while we can.

The food was delicious: steak, french fried potatoes, peas, tomatoes and mushrooms, sweet corn. The dessert was deep-dish apple pie spiced with cloves and cinnamon. The wine was French, chateau bottled. The cigarlets bore a familiar brand name.

Preston smoked, brooding, wishing that it were night so he could see alien constellations. He felt deflated. This place was too much like Earth. The gravity, the food and wine, the same plants even as far as he could tell. And the natives! Quiet, hygienic, dressed in leatherette and beads.

And yet was it so strange? A similar world would surely have a similar development. The chemical combination of aminoacids and DNA would combine to produce much the same sort of life. The local conditions would serve to mould it into familiar shapes. And the Kaltich would hardly bother with planets unsuitable to their kind of life.

This was a primitive world, he decided, much the same as Earth was a couple of hundred years ago. The Kaltich had discovered it, set up their Gates and engaged in trade. That was why so many things were familiar. They came from Earth. The Gate had come directly from Washington to here and so had the crates he had seen, the boxes of supplies.

Satisfied, he relaxed in his chair. The natives would only have a Stone Age culture. They couldn't make anything worth having and so could only exchange their services for essential items. A vacation planet, he thought. Something like the schloss but much larger. A world wide camping place where the Kaltich can pretend to rough it and, perhaps, do a little hunting.

Preston crushed out the cigarlet and lit

another. A group of deltas further down the veranda rose and walked toward the livery stable. They made no attempt to pay and no one seemed to bother. Why should they? thought Preston. Does a soldier pay for his food? That's true wealth, he told himself, the ability to take whatever you want when you want it. If nothing else the Kaltich were incredibly wealthy. On planets like this money was something they simply didn't bother to use.

But, on planets like this, he would never find the things for which he was searching.

He drew thoughtfully at his cigarlet, stiffening as a hand fell on his shoulder. He turned, looking upwards. The hand belonged to an alpha.

'Well,' he said, looking down at Preston. 'This is a stroke of luck. Mind if I join you?'

Preston gestured to an empty chair. 'Help yourself.'

'It's not often a man meets one of his own class in a place like this,' said the alpha sitting down. 'Name's Maddule.'

'Tulan,' said Preston. 'Jay Tulan.'

'Jay?' Maddox beamed. 'That puts us both in the upper half. I'm a Dee myself.'

'That's right.' They shook hands. Maddule was a man of comfortable middle-age. He wore the silver disc of a civilian and smelt a little of brandy. 'You're young,' he said looking at Preston. 'On your first tour of duty?'

Preston nodded.

Maddule sighed. 'I remember when I was about your age,' he said. 'Every time we put the Gate through I had to take a look. Must have been a hundred different places in that first tour alone. But we all do it,' he added. 'Like a kid with a new toy. The thrill wears off after a while.'

'I expect so,' said Preston cautiously.

'That's why I was surprised to see you,' continued Maddule. 'There's not much here to attract a young man. Not for another week or two at least. The buffalo will be along then,' he explained. 'They go south in the winter and back up north in the summer. Millions of them.'

'Buffalo?'

'That's right. Big ugly beasts. The

natives have fun in killing them. It's quite a spectacle in its way. They use horses to cut off a few and kill them with arrows and spears. Sometimes you'll get a young buck jump on one and kill it with a knife. That makes him popular with the women,' said Maddule dryly. 'Fortunately we don't need to prove ourselves in that way. You fond of shooting?'

'I've done a little,' said Preston.

'You could have some fun here in that case.' Maddule turned, waved at a waitress. 'Let's have a drink. You like brandy?'

'Yes,' said Preston. Luck, he thought, was still with him. Maddule was obviously a shade under the influence, loquacious and eager for company. The more he drank the more talkative he would become and the more Preston would learn. 'You come here often?'

'Not often.' Maddule poured, sipped, nodded his appreciation. 'Aside from the buffalo 1576 has little to offer. Easy targets, of course, if you like that sort of thing, but for real sport you should try 382. They're still in the dinosaur age,' he explained. 'Great ugly creatures with a brain the size of a nut. You need rocket rifles and lasers to bring them down.' He lifted his glass. 'Your health!'

They drank.

'But if you like setting yourself up against something really vicious, you want to try 891,' said Maddule, refilling the glasses. 'The insects are big on that one, damn big. Get yourself involved with a spider the size of a horse with a couple of wasps like vultures diving at your back and you won't forget it. Bottoms up!'

Preston reached for the bottle as Maddule set down his empty glass. 'How about the other worlds?'

'The M and R types?' Maddule shook his head. 'Nasty,' he said. 'Radioactivity can play the very devil with protoplasm. Those mutants — ' He shook his head. 'All right for the scientists, I suppose, but unless you like freaks they've nothing to offer. Except nightmares,' he added. 'More brandy?'

They had more brandy.

'Tell you what,' said Maddule. 'I could show you around a bit if you like. Cut a few corners. You've got the time?'

Preston nodded. This was what he'd been hoping for. 'I've got plenty of time,' he assured the other man. 'If it wouldn't put you to too much trouble I'd like to take advantage of your offer.' He smiled sycophantically. 'It's very good of you, sir. To be so generous, I mean.'

Maddule beamed. 'That's all right,' he said. A delta stood before the hitching rail. 'You,' Maddule called. 'Get me a hover car.' He reached for the bottle and smiled at Preston. 'Let's have one more for the road.'

Maddule drove the car, sending it weaving towards the Gate, droning up the ramp and jarring to a halt. 'Attention,' he called.

A panel slid open in the apparently solid wall. A gamma looked out. 'Sir?' he said respectfully. Beyond him Preston could see an elaborate instrument panel.

'Where does the Gate lead?'

'5354, sir.'

Maddule pursed his lips. 'Bronze age,' he said. 'Not much of interest unless you like gladiatorial games. Change to 1269,' he ordered. 'Readjust when passed.'

'At once, sir.' The gamma ducked back and did things to his instrument panel. Preston watched, learning nothing but that the man obviously controlled the operation of the Gate. He looked at the clear arch. It flickered. '1269, sir.'

Maddule waved and sent the hover car forward. Again the faint tingle. Preston wrinkled his nose as they glided down the ramp and away from the building. The air held a strong scent of seaweed and brine. Somewhere he could hear the sullen murmur of waves.

'If you're fond of seafood this is the place to be,' said Maddule. 'The continents never developed as they did elsewhere. It's a sea-based ecology. I've seen crabs twenty feet wide and clams ten. I can recommend it for fishing.' The car breasted a slight rise and Preston looked down at a wide beach, wave-capped shallows, an ocean dotted with massive clumps of weed. Manlike figures, tiny in the distance, dived and swam like a school of mermaids. 'Gilled,' said Maddule. 'They have to be. Even the young are born beneath the water. Sometimes it's hard to think of them as human.'

'Are they?'

'So the scientists say.' Maddule sent the car in a wide circle heading back towards the Gate. 'They're mammalian, anyway. Let's try 803.'

803 was a world of volcanoes, red glares at the horizon, drifting clouds of burning ash, and salamanderlike creatures which seemed impervious to flame. Preston studied a giant complex of what could only have been mining machinery attended by gnomish creatures disfigured by protective clothing.

'A meteor strike,' explained Maddule. 'A small asteroid must have split the surface and released the molten core. A long time ago now, of course. We find it handy for the extraction of selected metals. A worldwide smelting furnace,' he chuckled. 'Tough on those who work here but, well, you can't have everything.'

Which, thought Preston, couldn't be honestly said of the alpha. Maddule acted with the unconscious arrogance of a man who had never considered the possibility of being denied anything he wished. Not even the oldtime kings who had forced their subjects to treat them as if they had been divine could have dreamed of such absolute power. Worlds, for Maddule, were things to be seen as items of interest. At the Gates his word was law. In the caste system of the Kaltich the alphas were supreme.

'Well, my boy,' he said after a half-dozen more samplings, 'what now?'

Plans for the manufacture of the Gates, thought Preston. That and the secret of the longevity treatment. Those and a quick trip back to Earth. Instead he said, 'Well, sir, I'll leave that to you.'

'Nothing special that you'd like to see?'

Preston shook his head.

'No?' The alpha sent the car towards the opening of a Gate. 'Well,' he said as they halted. 'There's no place like home.'

'That's right,' said Preston.

'Sir?' The operator looked from his cubicle.

'One,' said Maddule curtly.

One, thought Preston. The home world

of the Kaltich, it could be nothing else. He was impatient to get away from his guide. I need a library, he thought. A place where I can find information on all these worlds. And details of the Gates. Then all I have to do is to walk in and ask for them. There's nothing an alpha can't have. As long as I'm in this uniform I can get away with anything. Simple, he told himself. It's going to be a piece of cake.

'Here we are,' said Maddule, and stepped from the car. Preston followed, staring at what he saw.

A wall pierced with doors. No opening or ramp or unloading bays. Nothing but a long row of Gates stretching to either side into and from which poured a steady stream of Kaltich. The terminus, he thought. The main junction. The heart of a transportation system which must be as complex as a city telephone exchange. But this is home, he reminded himself. You're supposed to be used to all this. Just thank the man and walk away as if you knew where you were going.

He smiled at Maddule and held out his hand. 'Thank you for showing me around, sir,' he said. 'I can't tell you how much I enjoyed it.'

'I'm sure that you did,' said Maddule, returning the smile. 'Going back on duty now?'

'Yes, sir.'

'Maybe we'll meet again. Where are you stationed?'

'1492,' said Preston quickly. 'Well, sir, thank you again.' He turned and walked away. The prickle between his shoulders warned him a split second before he heard the voice.

'Tulan! Halt or I'll drop you!'

Preston sprang to one side, running as he landed, heading for one of the openings opposite the Gates. He heard cries, a shout of warning, saw the startled eyes of a young girl dressed in blazing yellow. He tripped, fell, doubled with the searing agony of his left leg. Desperately he pounded at the knotted muscles in an effort to ease the cramp. Sweating, he looked up at Maddule. The alpha, no longer smiling, stared down at him. He held a thin tube in his left hand. He slipped it into his belt as two nulls came to stand at his side.

'I warned you,' he said. 'You should have obeyed.'

'Go to hell!' Preston gritted his teeth as he climbed to his feet. It was an effort to stand. 'Why?' he demanded. 'Why did you do that?'

'Did you really think,' Maddule asked coldly, 'that it was so easy to impersonate one of my class?'

9

There was a thin, high-pitched singing which ground at his bones like a dentist's drill, a sonic vibration which turned the world into a universe red with pain. It died and Preston saw again, felt the sweat running down his face and neck, the trembling of his hands. He took a deep breath, another, dragging air deep into his lungs. It was cool, sweet, smelling faintly of roses.

'That,' said the interrogator softly, 'was in the nature of a demonstration.' He was a gamma-alpha-null, a tall man, smooth with expressionless eyes and an implacable mouth. His hands were long, slender, sensitive instruments of his will. They rested on the surface of his desk close to a panel of buttons and tiny signal lights. As Preston watched a light changed from red to yellow to white. Dultar nodded as if with satisfaction. 'Let us understand each other,' he said. 'Here there can be no thought of resistance to the questions I may ask. Co-operation will gain you freedom from pain. And truth,' he added. 'I shall deal most severely with any attempt to lie.'

Preston didn't comment. He was still shaking from the sheer unexpectedness of the attack. He wiped the palms of his hands on the dull gray robe they had given him in exchange for his alpha uniform. His feet were bare. His hands were loosely manacled by a thin chain attached to cuffs on either wrist. The chain seemed fragile enough to snap at a jerk. He had tried it. The chain had not snapped but he had fallen groaning to the floor. The cuffs held electrical energy — disturbed, they grounded through the musculature of the body.

'Now,' said Dultar, 'I think we can progress. Your name?'

'Jay Tulan.'

'Please let us not waste time.' Dultar didn't raise his voice. He seemed, thought Preston, like a headmaster talking to a wayward pupil who didn't understand the power he was trying to defy. An Inquisitor faced with a heretic would have had the same unshakable conviction of superiority. 'I do not wish to hurt you more than is essential,' he said. 'I will ask you again. Your name?'

Preston scowled. 'I told you.'

'Tell me again.'

'Jay Tulan.'

A long, slender finger hovered over a button, then withdrew. 'I see that I must convince you that it is useless to lie,' said Dultar mildly. 'That is not your name and I know it.' He rose, crossed to a shelf, returned with a heavy volume bound in red. The cover bore the single initial J. 'This,' said Dultar, 'is a complete record of the Jay family. No Tulan is listed. It is obvious, therefore, that the name you give is an invention.'

Preston looked down at his hands. Luck, he thought. A man can only have so much luck. I used the last of mine when I picked on a name. How was I to know that, like the Chinese, the alphas and betas too, probably, put the surname first?

'You do not belong to the family of Jay,' continued the interrogator. 'Dee Maddule tells me that your ignorance was appalling. That, together with the fact that you carried a delta whip, made him suspicious. The clothes you were wearing, while genuine alpha garments, belonged to Zee Wayne. Where did you get them?'

Preston shook his head. This time the thin, high-pitched bone-aching sound drove him to the edge of consciousness. He hates me, he thought as it died away. To him, to all of the Kaltich, I've done the unforgivable. I've impersonated an alpha. A Catholic, he thought, would have felt much the same if I'd spat on the Pope.

Shaking, he stared about the room. Aside from the interrogator he was alone. The room itself was large, gleaming with surrogate marble, the floor of the same substance, rounded at the corners, rising to meet the walls. No place for dust. No place for mercy either.

'We are checking every Gate to discover the whereabouts of Alpha Zee Wayne,' said Dultar evenly. 'However, there are many Gates. It would help us both if you were to tell me where you obtained the garments.'

'I found them,' said Preston. A lamp on the panel winked red.

'Will you never learn that it is useless to lie?' Dultar rested his finger on a button. The sonic vibration focused on the chair in which Preston sat climbed higher up the scale. 'I could rupture every capillary in your body,' said Dultar emotionlessly. 'I could disintegrate your muscular co-ordination. I could burst you internally as I would a paper bag filled with water. Now, for the last time, where is Zee Wayne?'

'I don't know,' groaned Preston.

The lamp winked green.

The pain eased a little, faded completely as Dultar looked thoughtfully at his victim. 'I think you are dissembling,' he said. 'But I give you the benefit of the doubt. 'You met Zee Wayne?'

'No.' Preston had killed a stranger.

'You obtained the clothes from an alpha?'

Preston nodded.

'His name was Zee Wayne. I tell you this so you will understand the question. Where is Zee Wayne?'

'I don't know.'

The lamp winked green.

'Your name?'

'Preston. Martin Preston.'

'Where is Zee Wayne?'

'I don't know.' It was still the truth. I don't know where he is, thought Preston. Where does a man go when he dies? To Heaven? To Hell? Is he still in the Gate or buried outside? Canned for later use or hung out to dry. Tell the truth, he told himself. But don't tell all of it. Save yourself pain and answer the questions — and hope that this cold-blooded bastard doesn't ask the important one.

'Let us put the question in a different form,' said Dultar. He seemed blind to the obvious or, thought Preston, the concept that a man could actually kill one of the precious alphas for him simply did not exist. 'Where did you obtain the clothes?'

'On Earth,' said Preston.

And doubled in screaming agony.

★　★　★

He moved and discovered that his body obeyed his commands. He opened his eyes and stared at a low ceiling in which was set a glowing plate of luminous material. He raised his head and looked around. The shape of a cell, he thought, was always the same. Walls, bars, the bare necessities. A faucet protruded from one wall. He rose, crossed to it, drank greedily before he considered the prospect of drugged water. It didn't matter. It was too late for that.

'You must have had it bad, chum.'

Preston turned. He was not alone. A man sprawled in one corner of the cell. Like Preston he was dressed in grey, his wrists shackled by the thin chain. His face was sallow, gaunt with deprivation. Acid or some other corrosive had apparently eaten a livid scar into the side of his neck. The backs of his hands showed the same blotches.

'You had it bad,' he repeated, 'but not as bad as it could have been.' He gestured to the side of his neck. 'What you do? Bump into a gamma?'

Preston shook his head.

147

'I'm an epsilon,' volunteered the man. 'Name's Hughen.' He held out his hand. 'You?'

'Preston.' He ignored the outstretched hand. 'What are you in for?'

'I had a girl. A nice girl. We was going to get married. Had permission and everything. A delta saw her and wanted to use her. I didn't like the idea.' Hughen sucked in his cheeks. 'I knocked his hand off her arm,' he said. 'When he gave me the whip I kicked him where it hurt most. Stupidest damn thing I ever did,' he said. 'I lost the girl, most of my neck, everything. You?' Preston told him. Hughen whistled. 'Man, are you in trouble! An alpha! Where did you get the gear?'

Preston didn't answer. A stoolie, he thought. A pigeon. They must think I'm green putting me in here with him. Do they really expect me to spill all I know? If you do you're dead, he warned himself. As yet they don't know I killed that alpha. They can't think that way. To them a man wearing red is the next thing to God.

'You know the best thing to do in a

case like yours?' said Hughen. 'Tell them everything they want to know. Cooperate all along the line. That's what I'd do,' he said. 'That's what I did. Now I'm all fixed. They got me a job,' he explained. 'Another chance to make good. Tough, maybe, but it's more than I deserve. Not after kicking that delta. You play along with them and you'll be all right,' he summed up. 'Take my tip and tell them all they want to know.'

'Go to hell,' said Preston.

'They'll get it anyway,' his cell mate pointed out. 'They can use drugs to spread you wide open. They can take out your brain and put it in a case . . . ' He shuddered. 'It makes me feel sick when I think of all the things they can do.

'Yes,' said Preston.

'I'm telling you, that's all. Just telling you.'

Shut up, damn you, thought Preston. I don't need you to tell me the spot I'm in. So far I've been lucky. Somehow I got Dultar's goat. He lost his head and went too far. But it isn't over yet.

Irritably he began to pace the cell. It

was solid, broken only by the barred door. He went to it, leaned against it, tried to look down the corridor to either side. The bars were too close; he could see nothing but a short extension of the concrete wall. He examined the ceiling. Aside from the glowing plate it was as solid as the walls, the floor. He returned to the door and looked at the lock. It was, he guessed, electronically operated, controlled from a central point.

'If you're looking for a way out,' said Hughen, 'forget it. There isn't one.'

'No,' said Preston. And yet there had to be a way. He couldn't just sit here like a pig in a slaughterhouse waiting for them to come and empty his mind.

'Why don't you just sit down and relax?' said Hughen. He coughed. 'Listen,' he said apologetically. 'From what you told me you haven't much of a chance. Me, well I'm due to get out. If you want for me to carry a message or something?'

Preston turned from the door and looked at the man.

'A few words to the wife, maybe? Or the girl friend?' Hugen shrugged. 'I'm only trying to be helpful,' he said. 'You can trust me.'

'In a pig's eye,' said Preston. He turned, looking through the door as footsteps approached. Two null guards halted outside the cell. One gestured to Preston.

'You. Back against the wall.' He pointed to Hughen. 'You! Outside!' He stood back as the door slid open. 'Hurry!'

The epsilon obeyed. In the corridor he hesitated, looking at Preston. 'Take my advice,' he urged. 'Play it smart. Tell them all they want to know and maybe they'll go easy with you. After all,' he added. 'What can you lose?'

'Not much,' admitted Preston. He came close to the door, hoping to catch a fold of his robe between the lock and its jamb. One of the nulls stepped forward, thrusting out his stiffened arm.

'Back!' he snapped. 'Right back!'

Preston spat blood from his lacerated mouth.

★　★　★

Alone he gulped water, rinsing his mouth, taking stock of the situation. Aside from the robe he was naked. The robe and the chain. Again he examined it. The cuffs obviously contained the source of electrical energy together with the triggering mechanism. Gently he applied strain, hastily bringing his hands close together as pain stabbed at both wrists. Thoughtfully he stared at the glowing plate in the ceiling. It was just within reach and he ran the tips of his fingers around the edges. Nothing. His fingernails were too short and fragile to serve as screwdrivers. Again he looked at his manacles.

Water, he thought. The cuffs needn't be waterproof and, if they weren't, he could probably wreck the mechanisms, short them out in some way. Lifting the hem of his robe he tore at it with his teeth. The fabric, inferior plastic, yielded easily to the strain. Sliding the cuffs up each arm as far as they would go, he wrapped strips of the robe around each wrist, forcing the cuffs back over the crude insulation. Gritting his teeth he jerked. The chain snapped tight but held. Wincing, he closed his wrists together and tried again. The chain still held.

Wiping sweat from his forehead, he crossed to the faucet and looped the chain around the tap. Balancing on one leg, he pressed the other against the wall and thrust with all his strength. The tap bent a little, then the chain snapped with a vicious *ping*. Smoke rose from both wrists together with the stench of burning insulation. Quickly he turned on the faucet and held the cuffs in the stream of water. The smoke increased, something sparked, snapped, and the cuffs sprang open. Hastily he tore the burning plastic from his seared wrists. The stuff had softened with the heat, spreading and sticking like tar. When he ripped it off, skin tore free, leaving ugly raw patches seeping blood.

Cuffs and chain in hand he stepped towards the door and examined the lock. He fed the chain between the lock and jamb, making sure that it could move. He snapped shut the cuffs about the lock and the opposing bar, then tugged at the chain. It grew red, softened, fell in molten droplets. The cuffs smoked as they released their energy into the lock. Preston jerked at the door. It opened. He stepped from the cell.

Outside, a corridor studded with barred doors and lit by a row of flowing plates in the ceiling ran to either side. The nulls had taken Hughen to the right. There would be a gate of some kind, an officer on duty, perhaps several. If he managed to get to the gate he would get no further. He ran along the corridor in the opposite direction halting when he saw the grill of an air vent. He thrust his fingers into the mesh and pulled. His position was awkward, the leverage all wrong. He gripped harder and swung up his legs, setting his feet to either side of the grill. Quickly, before gravity could overcome his limited strength, he heaved, using the full power of leg and shoulder muscles. The grill bent, cutting into his fingers, suddenly tearing free. He fell heavily. From one of the cells a face peered.

'Hey! What's going on out there? Hey, you!'

'Shut your mouth!' snarled Preston. He flung the grill at the cell door and sprang towards the opening. It gave onto a narrow ventilation shaft. He dived down it, tearing his robe on slight projections, choking as he stirred up clouds of accumulated dust. He came to a junction and hesitated. Wetting a finger he held it before his face and felt a slight coldness on one side. Without hesitation he moved towards it, hurrying, clawing forward in the darkness, intent only on gaining as much distance as possible before the nulls commenced their search.

The dust, he knew, would make it a simple race against time.

The guards would have lights. They would spot his tracks. All they would have to do would be to follow them. His only hope lay in getting out of the ventilation system and finding somewhere safe to hide before they caught up with him. He swore as his head crashed against a barrier. Blindly he felt to either side. One shaft led upwards, others to left and right. He forced his head into the one leading upwards, groping with his hands. Without conscious thought he began to climb, wedging himself against the side of the narrow shaft. He froze at the echo of voices.

'This way. Damn! I've got blood on my uniform.'

'Makes it easier for us to follow.'

'Get moving there!'

Galvanised, he surged upwards. He felt open space around his head and a slight pressure of air. Twisting from the shaft he turned, keeping the faint wind at his back, diving down an unsloping tube, crawling with elbow and knee motions, unable to lift himself higher. The tube narrowed still more and he felt the scrape of metal on back and stomach. Soon it pressed against his shoulders. He hesitated, wondering whether to retreat, then saw a flash of light ahead. Extending his arms he thrust himself forward with his feet. The light vanished as he touched a grill, replaced by a soft moonglow, barely strong enough to see the barrier. Bracing his feet he pushed, snarling as his bare feet slid on the smooth metal. Hunching his knees he drove himself headfirst against the metal. It yielded a little. Wedging himself in the shaft, he smashed against it with his shoulder. The grill was thin, strictly ornamental. It gave and he fell after it.

★　★　★

He was in a bathroom, the floor thickly carpeted, the furnishings luxurious. A soft glow came from above a wall mirror and he looked at a savage, smeared with dirt and blood, dressed in rags and with burning eyes. He turned and the savage turned with him. The place held a tub, a shower, a toilet, washbasin and bidet. Hunting through a cabinet he found a nailfile ten inches long. He rammed the blunt end into a cake of soap and stepped toward the door. The light in the bathroom had gone on, then off, so it was logical to assume that someone was in the other room. Perhaps more than one, but there was no time to be cautious. Preston jerked open the door and found himself in a bedroom. Someone was in the bed.

'What — ?'

He sprang forward, hitting with the edge of his hand, almost killing before he realized it was a woman. Barely in time he softened the blow, turning the vicious chop into a relentless pressure on the carotids. The woman sighed as she slumped into unconsciousness. A door clicked in another room.

Preston waited, crude knife poised as he crouched beside the door. Nothing. The click had signaled a departure not an arrival. Quickly he checked the wardrobe and found it full of feminine garments. A second bedroom opened from the first and this time the clothes belonged to a man. A gamma. Preston shed his rags and struggled into a uniform which was two sizes too small. Sweating with pain he forced his feet into the shoes then hobbled into a second bathroom, a twin of the first. He washed, combed his hair, found a cream which removed his stubble. Carefully he wiped himself dry, resisting the impulse to run and run and keep on running. First he had to have a plan. And no plan would be worth anything unless he managed to appear respectable. Somehow he had to get out of the building and away from the hunt.

Just let me keep moving, he told himself, and I'll be all right. Once they've lost the trail they'll have the hell of a job to find it again. No more mistakes, he promised. No more taking things for granted. And, he thought grimly, no more interrogation. That above all.

Taking a deep breath he left the bedroom. The outer rooms were empty; he made sure of that with a quick inspection. Some bottles stood on the table and he helped himself to brandy. The spirit warmed his stomach and he poured himself a second drink while he stood, thinking.

I mustn't forget anything, he thought. Luck like I've had can't last. Am I dressed right? The whip? The belt? The uniform cap? Do I look right? Indolent. A little bored and more than a little arrogant. What's my name? Where am I going? Where have I come from? He swallowed the brandy and paused, looking at drawn curtains. A window, he thought. The first I've seen. A chance to look at this world of the Kaltich. It could help.

He drew the curtains.

He looked at sky, land and, in the far distance, the incredible bulk of a building rising like a mountain from a featureless plain. A truncated cone wreathed in cloud so vast that he could only guess at the size.

'Kalthis,' said a voice from behind. A smooth, hatefully familiar voice. 'That isn't a window, of course. Did you think it was?'

Preston turned, slowly, the hand holding the crude knife at his side, shielding it from view with his body. Dultar stood a few yards distant. He was armed with a small pistol which he kept levelled in his left hand. His right toyed with his whip.

'Not a window,' repeated the interrogator. 'A simulated projection. But look at the ground. Can you appreciate what has been done in so short a time? New soil from a dozen worlds to replace our sterile loam. Soon we shall have trees and grass and flowers blooming where only slag existed before. This interests you?'

'Very much.' Preston turned a little more, slowly, carefully. In his hand the knife slid through his fingers until he gripped the point of the file. 'How did you find me?'

'We traced you. Once we had you trapped there was no immediate hurry.' Dultar looked at Preston's borrowed clothes. 'You seem to have a penchant for imposture. What is your real class?'

'Ordinary man.'

'An epsilon?' Dultar raised his eyebrows. 'Surely not. How could a common white show such initiative? Such disregard for rank? You interest me,' he mused. 'We shall have many sessions together.'

'I don't think so,' said Preston.

The interrogator shrugged. 'You have no choice in the matter. I am rather looking forward to our talks,' he said. 'I shall extract every grain of information you carry. In time I will have the entire truth. I misjudged you before,' he admitted. 'I allowed you to inflame my temper. Anger is not good in one of my profession. But,' he added meaningfully, 'I shall not make the same mistake again. You will not escape so easily. Soon, my enigma, you will be begging me to grant you the release of death.'

Preston threw his weapon.

It was clumsy, but it was pointed and weighted and that was enough. Dultar made a strangled sound as the point of the file ripped into his eye, the weight of the soap driving it through the socket into the brain. He threw up his head, already dead, reflex constricting his finger as he fell.

The pistol flamed into stammering life.

Preston felt a giant hand smash into his chest, heard an idiot hammer shatter the facsimile window, saw an invisible pick gouge at the wall. He fell, rolled, stared at the blood gushing from his chest.

Oddly there was no pain.

I'm dead, he thought. He shot me, smashed my heart, ripped my lungs. He coughed and red sprayed over the green he wore. He looked up and saw running nulls. They seemed to be dwindling, shrinking, falling back even as they ran.

He knew they could never arrive in time.

10

It was comfortable to be dead. There was
no pain, no fatigue, no hunger or thirst.
There was nothing but a blissful sensation
as if floating on a cloud. I'm in Heaven,
thought Preston. I was shot and killed
and now I'm in Heaven. But Heaven was
a noisy place. Someone was talking and
he wished they wouldn't.

'Wake up! Please wake up! You must
wake up!'

A woman's voice, he decided. Or rather
that of a girl. Somehow it lacked the tonal
strength which came with maturity. A
young girl, he thought. A frightened
young girl. But frightened of what?

'You must wake up!' The voice held a
note of desperation. 'Please wake up!
Please!'

'Why should I?' said Preston. If it was a
dream he was enjoying it. 'Stop bothering
me.'

'You're awake! Good. Now listen. I

know that you can hear me. Pretend to be worse than what you are. It's very important that you make out you're really sick. On no account let them move you. I'll be back.'

Then silence and time for thought, for exploration.

He wasn't deaf or, if he was, the girl had spoken mind-to-mind. Telepathic? Preston didn't think so. The voice had been too sharp, too precise for that. So he wasn't deaf and, apparently, he wasn't in Heaven.

Perhaps, incredibly, he wasn't even dead.

Not dead, he thought. Injured, dying maybe, but not dead. Not yet at least, he qualified. But if Dultar has his way I won't be enjoying life for long. Then he remembered, the gamma, the crude knife shearing into his brain, the wild spray of shots and the running nulls.

Then nothing.

Cautiously he tried to lift his arms and found they wouldn't obey. His legs the same. His head refused to move. His eyes? He felt terror as he stared at darkness knowing that his eyes were open and that he should be seeing something, anything. He opened his mouth and yelled his panic. His tongue, at least, seemed to be working. He called again, louder. A third time.

'Steady!' Another voice, masculine, hard, sharp, devoid of patience. 'There's no need for that.'

'I'm blind,' said Preston. 'I can't see.'

'Not with the mask on, you can't,' the voice agreed. Preston felt something fumble at the side of his head and cool air struck his cheeks. Blinking, he looked up at a man dressed in delta blue. 'Is that better?'

Preston nodded.

'What's the matter with your voice?'

'I . . . ' Preston swallowed, feigning huskiness. 'It's all right, I guess.' He rolled his eyes, afraid to turn his head, 'What happened? Where am I?'

'You were shot,' said the delta curtly. 'The nulls applied emergency treatment and passed you through for medication. I am in charge of you while you are here.'

'You operated on me?'

'No. A local did that. You had a complete heart-lung regraft and have been in accelerated healing. Subjective time,' the delta explained. 'Speeded metabolism. A week to you was an hour to us. It's over now,' he added. 'A few hours for orientation and you'll be fit enough to move.'

Preston took a deep breath. 'Not dead?'

The delta shook his head. 'Not yet,' he said grimly. 'Not until you've answered quite a few questions.' He looked sharply at Preston. 'Is anything wrong?'

'I . . . my . . . ' Preston let his mouth gape, rolling his eyes upwards. 'Feel faint,' he gasped. 'Weak — '

'Scared,' said the delta. 'You've got a lot to answer for and you know it. You're scared, not weak.' He moved out of sight. 'Scared,' he said again and there was the click of a closing door.

Scared, thought Preston. Maybe so, but I've reason to be weak and you just try to prove that I'm not. He remembered the strange, whispering voice. Strapped as he was in a hospital cot, it offered a slender ray of hope. Someone knew about him and cared enough to communicate. And the instructions were simple to follow. He did feel weak. Shaken at the thought of what had happened.

You died, he told himself. The way you were shot you could have done nothing else. But the nulls got to you in time. They did something and sent you here. New heart and lungs, he thought. A major regraft. They hooked your brain to a bypass machine to feed it with oxygenated blood. They opened your chest as if you'd been a suitcase and exchanged the damaged organs as if they had been mechanics switching a set of injectors on a hover car.

He thought of Hilda Thorenson. She could have done it, he told himself. A lot of surgeons on Earth could have done it. It isn't anything unusual. Just a replacement. Back home it would have cost you a fortune — here you've had it done for free.

But, he thought, the payment would come later. And it would be a hell of a price to pay. The condemned man, he mused. You've got to cure him before you can kill him and never mind the cockeyed logic. Only here there would be logic and it wouldn't be a simple matter of killing. He would take a long, long time to die and, even when dead, there would be no guarantee that he would stay that way.

They'll torture me to death, he decided. And then revive me to torture me again. Over and over until they've learned all there is to know. And what then? STAR would be made to suffer and so would Earth. Turned into a charred ruin, perhaps, a ghastly example and a warning to others never to raise their hands against the Kaltich. And he would be a small part of that example. A living, screaming, suffering scrap of humanity used to show others what to expect if they disobeyed.

No, he thought bleakly, this isn't Heaven.

The cot was in a small room which was glassed down one end so as to give full visibility from outside. The door was set in the glass. When they had eased the restraints Preston could see other doors facing his own across a wide corridor.

Most of the rooms seemed empty but a few held patients, some barely visible beneath a mass of machinery. Life-support systems, he supposed. Mechanisms to control the speeded metabolisms. Feeding, if nothing else, would be a problem in such a condition.

The corridor was rarely empty. Orderlies dressed in pink walked up and down the passage. Doctors in their lime green hustled by. Women in powder blue were nurses. Red green and blue, thought Preston. Familiar colours but not Kaltich shades. They can't wear white, he told himself. Only the underlings, the serfs do that and these people aren't serfs. They're skilled medical personnel. But they wear distinguishing colours.

He wondered if they were Kaltich at all.

He asked his doctor, a thin-faced man with short-cropped hair and a brusque manner. The lime green of his clothing gave him a sallow, unhealthy expression. His nails and person were scrupulously clean. He glanced to where a screen was set in the ceiling.

169

'I am not here to answer your questions,' he said sharply. 'You are my patient and it is my duty to see that you get fit and well in as short a time as possible. And I must confess I am baffled at your continuing weakness. It should have passed by now.'

'It hasn't,' Preston insisted.

'You were naturally in deep shock,' said the doctor. 'And these burns on your wrists didn't help.' He pursed his lips, thinking. 'We'll give it a little longer,' he decided. 'To the maximum degree of tolerance at least. After that we shall have to consider the psychological aspect.'

'Thank you, Doctor,' said Preston dryly. 'I appreciate your concern. But I'm not a slab of beef on a butcher's counter. Neither am I a culture on one of your agar plates. Nor,' he added pointedly, 'am I a criminal in your sense of the word. I am a man and therefore curious.'

'What do you know of agar plates?'

'Enough. One of my best friends is a doctor. A surgeon. She contends that the more a patient knows of his condition the more cooperative he is able to be.

Frustration is bad medicine, Doctor. So why not answer? Are you of the Kaltich?'

'No.'

'You just work for them?'

'We work for all who need our skills.'

'Your medical skills, of course,' said Preston. He frowned, thinking. 'Do you mean,' he said carefully, 'that anyone, no matter what race, creed or social standing, can come to you for medical treatment?'

The doctor was stiff. 'Naturally. What else?'

Dedicated, thought Preston. The idealised conception of a true medical service. The spirit of Florence Nightingale, Pasteur, a thousand others. All the men and women who risked and gave their lives for the purpose of easing human suffering. And, apparently, a dedication unsullied by considerations of material gain.

'This world,' he said abruptly. 'It isn't the home of the Kaltich?'

'No.'

'But they come here,' said Preston. 'They all come here. Thousands and millions of people. The longevity treatment,' he said, with a sudden flash of insight. 'It's yours. You developed it. You issue it.'

'You are talking too much,' said the doctor. 'You must not overexert yourself.'

Millions, thought Preston, shaken at the concept. Millions from Earth alone. And what of the other worlds? It has to be a worldwide culture, he decided. It can't be anything less. A whole planet devoted to the pursuit of medical knowledge. Laboratories instead of factories. Hospitals instead of hotels. The breeding of helpful bacteria instead of delving for minerals. But where do they get their raw supplies? Their food? The things they must have?

It was a foolish question. Think of Earth, he told himself. Remember the uncounted billions poured out on defence, the endless stream of wealth wasted on weapons and means to kill. Think of all that money channelled into medicine. Think of what we could have accomplished had we not followed the god of war.

The doctor finished his examination,

held his hands in a stream of warm, antiseptic air, looked down at Preston. 'I'm removing the rest of the restraints,' he said. 'You can do without them now. However, I must warn you not to get up and most certainly not to leave this room.' Again he glanced at the ceiling. 'If you need anything that button will summon assistance. If you are bored that control will provide entertainment.'

'I'll remember that,' said Preston. 'Doctor, I'd like to thank you.'

The man raised his eyebrows.

'For saving my life,' said Preston.

'I did not save your life,' corrected the doctor. 'The men who gave you the emergency treatment did that. Saved your intelligence at least,' he added. 'Do you realize just how long the brain can be deprived of oxygen?'

'Three minutes,' said Preston. 'A maximum of five.'

'So you know that?' The doctor pursed his lips. 'I had been given to understand — but never mind. You are correct. We can provide means to throw the brain into a temporary stasis. We can even provide a vehicle to carry oxygen direct to the deprived cells. A bacteria,' he explained. 'Injected into the skull it has an affinity for the cortex and will provide the missing gas for up to fifteen minutes. But, of course, its use rarely necessary. It takes so little time to get through a Gate.'

'If you have one handy,' said Preston.

'But naturally,' said the doctor. And left.

★　★　★

Preston stared at the screen set into the ceiling. A television screen, he thought, but he knew that it was more than that. A spy ear, he told himself. Somewhere a man sits watching every move I make, listening to every word I say. He guessed that every cubicle was so equipped for the sake of automated nursing. But I'm special, he reminded himself. I bet that I've got a watcher all to myself.

Restlessly he moved on the cot. He felt like a fly pinned to a board, a germ under a microscope. Even if he left the room where could he go? Hospitals had the same attributes as prisons — everyone wore a distinctive uniform. How far would he get dressed in a loose robe of silver grey?

He touched the control the doctor had pointed out. It was double, one graduated dial within another. He twisted the inner one and heard music coming from somewhere beneath his pillow. Thoughtfully he returned it to its original setting and twisted the outer dial. Light and colour filled the picture which seemed to be that of a butcher dissecting a steer. A mass of red and yellow tissue served as a background to the gleaming silver of instruments.

' . . . at work on a routine case of pancreas transfer. You will note that Doctor Beynon is using a Symond scalpel which not only cuts but temporarily seals the wound so that there is no hampering flow of blood. Temporarily, because of the need for free blood flow during later suturing. This, obviously, puts a time limit on the operation and no surgeon who has not sufficient skill to work at speed should use this particular instrument. If, for reasons of . . . '

Preston twisted the control. The soft voice died to be replaced by another together with accompanying picture. This time it was to do with the removal of a brain tumor. Another attempt resulted in detailed instructions on how to remove a kidney. A fourth had a professor talking about the lower intenstine.

Lectures, thought Preston. Tuition. Recorded operations constantly broadcast so as to give everyone the benefit of vicarious experience. Natural enough on a world dedicated to medical care. Like the Christians, he thought. In the Middle Ages almost everything had some reference to religion. Irritably he turned the switch and this time caught a play. Settling back he watched it. Watching, he frowned.

The locale was Europe, the characters spoke of Austria, France, Germany and England. The action took place in Vienna. The hero was a small excitable man named Ignaz Phillipp Semmelweis. The play presented him much as a medieval mystery play would present Christ. He was the redeemer, the man with the message, the opener of the way.

Which, admitted Preston, was true enough. In 1847 Semmelweis had reached the conviction that cleanliness was essential to the practice of medicine. Knowing nothing of microbes, he had the pragmatic certainty that disease could be transferred by contaminated matter from the dead to the living and from those diseased to those who were well. His solution, that all doctors and students should wash their hands in chlorine water between examinations of patients, was verified by his own amazing success in reducing the mortality rate of those under his direct care.

A simple thing, mused Preston. A thing every child knows almost by instinct. The need to wash before touching anything which should be kept clean. Semmelweis proved the necessity. In return he was viciously derided by his own profession.

Thirty years, thought Preston, watching the screen. Thirty wasted years before the message Semmelweis had given had been accepted in the light of new discoveries. Would those years have made all that difference? Perhaps, he told himself.

Western civilization had been poised on the springboard of scientific progress. It was the time of new discoveries, new inventions, an enlarging of the horizons of the mind. Had that wealth and enthusiasm been channelled into the field of medicine, who could guess at the progress which could have been made? But those thirty years had been wasted. Semmelweis had not been heeded. And who could tell what genius had been lost on dirty operating tables or in the filthy conditions reigning in the maternity wards of famous hospitals?

★ ★ ★

Night came, a darkening of lights and dimming of visibility. Little sounds died, orderlies moved like pink ghosts down the corridor, the smooth life of the hospital, in this section at least, slowed in obedience to the basic animal-rhythm of day and night. Preston tried to sleep and found it impossible. He stirred and tried the television. A swirl of kaleidoscopic colour and a soft, hypnotic voice — ' . . . relaxed.

So relaxed, so sleepy, so detached. Just look at the colours and let yourself go. Sink deep into the wonderful colours, sink, sink . . . relax . . . sleep . . . '

Other channels were the same. The programme, he guessed, was piped, selected to a particular audience. Patients with insommnia were more easily treated with hypnotism than with drugs.

Irritably he turned, half tempted to get up and see what could be done, knowing that any such action would be an invitation to disaster. He had to pretend that he was too weak to stand so that, when and if the right time came, he would at least have the advantage of surprise.

'Are you awake? Please tell me if you are awake.' The voice was familiar, he had heard it before. Preston stayed motionless as the voice whispered from beneath his pillow. The radio, he thought. Someone has tapped the wire. Or, he corrected, maybe someone wants me to think exactly that. 'Are you awake?' The voice was a little petulant. 'Answer if you are.'

Preston yawned, rolled, hunched the

covers so as to cover his mouth. A man trying hard to get to sleep. 'I'm awake,' he said. 'I can hear you.'

'Good. Do not move or show surprise. When you answer do not move your lips or speak too loudly. Everything you say and do is being monitored.'

'I know,' he whispered. 'Who are you?'

'Please listen. There are things that we must know. First, what is your name?'

'Preston. Martin Preston.' The Kaltich knew that already, he was giving nothing away.

'You killed a man. What was his name?'

'Dultar. A gamma. An interrogator of the Kaltich.' They knew that too.

'Anyone else?'

Preston didn't answer. So that's it, he thought. It didn't end with Dultar. It will never end. Aloud he said, 'I don't understand what you mean. Do you think I go around killing people?'

'The Kaltich have a special interest in you,' whispered the voice. 'We would like to know just why.'

'Are you curious or do you have a reason?'

180

'Not so loud,' warned the voice then, 'We have a reason. If you are important to them you could be important to us. If so, we are willing to help you. But first we must be certain that the effort will be justified. Why are the Kaltich so concerned?'

'They think I know something,' said Preston. He hesitated, then mentally shrugged. The voice could be telling the truth or it could be a part of an involved trap. In either case he had nothing to lose. 'They caught me impersonating an alpha. I guess to them that's a pretty serious crime. They want to make me pay for it.'

'And the man whose clothes you were wearing,' said the voice shrewdly. 'Did you kill him?'

The big one, he thought sickly. The one question he'd hoped to avoid. Did they have the bed wired as a lie-detector? Were they even now waiting, leaning forward perhaps, eager to learn whether or not he had done that unspeakable thing?

'No,' he said. The voice hadn't specified which clothes. When shot he'd been wearing the uniform of a gamma and he hadn't killed the man. He hadn't even seen him. The truth, he told himself. Always tell the truth — or at least your version of it. To hell with the Kaltich and their tricks.

'You are cautious,' said the voice. 'We can admire you for that. And you are a little afraid. That too we can understand. The Kaltich inspire fear. And yet you have shown that fear to be an empty thing. We could learn from you. More important you may have something we could use. But we must be certain that you are not a plant.'

That makes two of us, thought Preston. 'Listen,' he said urgently. 'I don't know who you are but you seem to know all about me. I killed a Kaltich. A gamma. You must know what that means. Do you think they would allow one of their number to be killed just to set up a decoy?'

The voice was cold. 'They might.'

'Then you know little about them. They take. They never give. They promise but never perform. As a race they're selfish. As individuals even more so. I want to get out of here,' said Preston. 'Out and back to my own world. Can you help me do that?'

'Perhaps.'

'If you can't or if you don't want to then keep out of my life,' he snapped. 'I've had enough sadism to last me as long as I'm going to live. In other words,' he emphasised, 'put up or shut up. Understand?'

Silence.

'All right,' said Preston savagely. 'If that's the way you want it. Goodnight!'

He felt his hands clench until the nails dug into his palms. I handled it right, he assured himself. The only way I could handle it. Beg and they would have got suspicious. Plead and it would have been the same. Defy them and maybe they'll get curious. They think I'm tough, he thought. I couldn't disappoint them.

Them?

He knew who they were, who they had to be. It was inevitable, he thought. In a world like this they couldn't help but be strong. Just like Earth, he told himself. We have STAR. There must be similar organizations on other worlds. On every world that had pride and the ability to see ahead. That's where the voice came from. That's who is going to help you escape. The only ones really equipped to do it.

If they decided to do it.

Seconds dragged into minutes. He began to sweat and had to force himself to lie still. They've got to come to me, he thought. If I try to contact them they'll run like mice. There's nothing you can do now but wait. And wait. And wait.

'We have decided,' said the voice. 'We will arrange to help you. It is imperative that you follow every order without question and without delay. Is this understood?'

'Yes.'

'You will be notified.'

'Wait!' He swallowed choosing his words. 'Just who are you?' he said carefully. 'I think I should know.'

'Certainly. We are GERM.'

'Germ?'

'G.E.R.M.,' said the voice patiently. 'General Earth Resistance Movement. Goodnight.'

GERM, he thought, rolling over onto his back and looking thoughtfully at the screen. A good name for a medical world. An appropriate name. He could appreciate the innuendo. GERM, the disease which could weaken and even destroy the Kaltich. GERM.

General Earth Resistance Movement.

He stiffened in the bed.

Earth?

11

On the smooth floor the rubber wheels of the trolley made not even a whisper of sound. Preston lay as ordered, rigid, stiff as a corpse, motionless as the vehicle moved, turned, dropped, moved to drop again into what he guessed must be the basement of the building. A door closed. Light squinted his eyes as the sheet was jerked from his face. A woman wearing green looked down at him. She had red hair and blue eyes. Her age, he guessed, couldn't have been more than twenty-five.

'Hello.' She smiled and held out her hand. 'I'm Sylvia Meecham.' Her voice was the one which had come from beneath his pillow. Preston sat upright and took her hand. It was hard, firm with developed muscle, a surgeon's hand.

'I'm glad to meet you,' he said, and added. 'I mean that more than perhaps you realise.'

'Let us hope that you have no reason to change your mind.' She threw him a bundle of clothing, an orderly's uniform plus soft-soled shoes. 'Get off the trolley and change into these.' She watched as he stripped, unembarrassed by his nakedness, then turned to the two men in pink who had handled the vehicle. 'Trouble?'

One of them shook his head. 'None. Everything went as planned.'

'Good. You'd better get back now. I'll handle it from here.'

They left. Preston finished dressing and looked at the girl. 'Listen,' he said. 'There's something I've got to ask you. About GERM. What — '

She interrupted, glancing at her watch. 'Later.'

'But — '

'Later. Now please follow me.'

Preston shrugged. It was her game and he had to play by her rules but, he told himself, I'm going to get to the bottom of this and soon. If she won't answer then perhaps her friends will.

'Hurry,' said the girl.

'Coming,' said Preston and stepped

through the door into an anatomist's nightmare.

He was surrounded by tiers of crystal vats in which rested lungs, spleens, kidneys, livers, stomachs, glands, fathoms of intestines, miles of nerve-fibre. Eyeballs floating like watchful marbles. Hearts beat with a sleepy rhythm. Bone looked like yellow-white sticks of celery immersed in nutrient fluids. Every part of the human body grew quietly in the rows of containers. Every part but a brain.

'That is the one spare part we cannot supply,' said the girl, guessing his thoughts. 'We can grow a cortex, of course, but doing so gives rise to various problems. Intelligence,' she explained. 'Awareness of self. We could use cerebal matter as the control nexus of organotic servomechanisms. We could even produce a brain with a surrogate personality but what would be the point? If you were to die,' she said, 'really die, which means the destruction of the brain, what good would it do you for us to supply a new brain with its own personality?'

'None,' he admitted. 'But I am

surprised that you have such ethical considerations. Surely, to you, a body is what a hover car is to a mechanic?'

'True,' she said. 'But only as far as we deal in organic replacements. The brain is in a different category. We do not tamper with the seat of intelligence. We can rebuild a brain,' she admitted, 'but always there is the problem of personality. Have you seen a zombie?'

Preston shook his head.

'A living, walking, breathing creature. But one without conscious intelligence. Worse than a moron. Worse than insane. A thing. The brain serving only to coordinate the functions of the body. Horrible!'

'I'll take your word for it,' said Preston. He had, he thought, taken her word for quite a lot but, as yet, he had nothing to complain about. 'What happens now?' he demanded. 'I mean, won't the Kaltich get annoyed when they find I'm gone? Won't they guess you had something to do with it?'

She smiled, obviously amused. 'Why should they? You are dead,' she said. 'A body now lies in your cot. Soon a doctor will examine you and pronounce you officially extinct.'

'But the monitoring device? Won't they have spotted the exchange?'

'No.' She stepped past the last tier of vats and led the way down a corridor. 'We run this hospital,' she pointed out. 'At the critical time an adjustment was made in the circuitry. The waiting Kaltich noticed nothing. There was no reason for him to guess that he was watching another patient. After you had left the adjustment was rectified. The examining doctor, of course, is a member of GERM.'

It made sense, thought Preston. If you wanted to build up a resistance group what better place than in a hospital? The staff already worked in unison, had a common loyalty, were used to emergencies and sudden effort. He guessed that the body which had taken his place had been made to resemble himself.

'They won't like it,' he said. 'The Kaltich, I mean. They're not going to like it at all.'

Sylvia shrugged.

'They can be nasty,' he warned.

'Yes,' she said quietly. 'We've learned that in the past. Why else do you think we have GERM?'

* * *

The passage ended in a door. Beyond it was a small room containing three men, a chair, a cabinet of drugs and instruments and a large wall clock. One of the men pointed to the chair. 'Sit down.'

Preston sat, rising immediately when he saw one of the other men coming toward him with something glittering in his hand. 'Now wait a minute,' he protested.

'Sit down,' repeated the first man. 'Jarl. Max.'

'All right,' said Preston. He sat down and looked at the woman. She stood silently behind the obvious leader of the group. 'What's going to happen?'

'No talking,' said the man. 'Just keep sitting and do as you're told.'

Preston took a deep breath, sprang upright and spun so as to stand behind the chair. He gripped it, lifted it, poised it to throw.

'No!' said the woman sharply. 'Don't be a fool!' She looked at the leader. 'Tell him, John. Explain.'

'We've got to find out if you're genuine,' said the man reluctantly. 'Now put down that chair and relax so that we can get on with it.'

Preston hesitated.

'You've got a choice,' said John. 'You do things our way or we kill you. This isn't a game,' he added. 'This is for real. Now put down that chair and stop wasting time.'

'It's my time,' said Preston.

'Maybe, but it's our necks.' John lifted his hand. He held a gun. 'I'm giving you one last chance. Put down that chair or I'll drop you.'

He wasn't bluffing. Preston put down the chair and sat in it. Jarl came towards him holding a hypogun. The blast of air made a small sound as it sent a charge of drugs through the pink uniform, through the skin and fat into the bloodstream. Preston leaned back, relaxing as he looked at the clock. The hands pointed to 3:37. He blinked. The hands now pointed

192

to 4:26. He looked around. Aside from Sylvia and John the room was empty.

'You're clear,' said John. 'Either that or you've had one of the best preconditioning jobs in history. I'm gambling that you're genuine.'

'It's no gamble,' said Preston. His mouth was dry, either from talking or from the effects of the drug. 'I'm not working for the Kaltich. You've got nothing to worry about as far as I'm concerned. In fact,' he added, 'I don't know what you've got to worry about at all. Couldn't you just tell the Kaltich where to get off?'

'No,' said the woman.

'Yes,' said the man.

'Make up your mind,' said Preston. He swallowed to ease the dryness of his throat. He felt irritable, weaker than he'd expected. And why not? You've had a major operation, he told himself. Even though you've had weeks of subjective time in which to heal you've still been in bed. Lifting that chair had been a stupid thing to have done, he decided. And yet he'd had to do it. At least it had made them respect him a little.

'We can't do without them,' said Sylvia. 'Not now.'

'We could if we really wanted to,' said the man. He looked at Preston. 'You know how it is,' he said. 'A world divided. One part wants pure freedom — the other wants what the Kaltich has to offer. Even GERM isn't wholly united.'

Neither is STAR, thought Preston wearily. Neither is UNO. Neither is any group with more than a few members. Maybe that's a good thing. If everyone thought alike where would they be? Under, he decided. Under this or under that or under something else. But under.

'So what are you working for?' he asked. 'To get rid of the Kaltich?'

They nodded.

'Then why not just kick them out? Refuse to play? They need you more than you need them,' he said. 'You hold the top hand. You can supply what they need and you can always threaten to cut off that supply.'

No, he thought, it can't be as simple as that. They would have their own hospitals, their own medical personnel. He

194

remembered the tremendous building he had seen in the facsimile window. They must have everything, he decided. They would never let themselves become dependent on any one world.

'It isn't as simple as that,' said Sylvia Meecham. 'We need the Kaltich or,' she qualified, 'we need what they bring us. Divergent types from which to grow our spare parts. Radioactive isotopes and rogue tissues from the M and R worlds. Primitive cellular organisms — a thousand other things. We are a hospital culture,' she pointed out. 'A world devoted to medical care. A society geared to the endless treatment of the sick. It is the reason for our existence.'

And, he thought bleakly, your Achilles' heel. What was the good of a planetful of doctors if they had no patients? How could they utilise their learning if there was no one on which to operate? An army has to fight if it is to stay an army. A man must do what he has trained himself to be good at. Rob him of the opportunity and you take away the meaning of his life.

'They control the Gates,' said Sylvia.

'We need them. The Gates, not the Kaltich, but we have to take one to get the other. Eighty-three years,' she said. 'That's how long the Kaltich have been here. Eighty-three years during which our society has expanded only in one direction. Can you guess how many doctors we have now? How many orderlies, nurses, laboratory workers? You saw some of our spare parts. Well, this is only a small hospital. The Kaltich use it for their personal use, which is why they sent you here. That's why we rescued you. That's — '

'Just a minute,' said Preston. He rested his aching head between his hands. Doctors, he thought bitterly. How selfish can they get? I'm sick but she doesn't give a damn. Aloud he said, 'Eighty-three years. That would put it just after the war.'

John frowned. 'Which war?'

'World War Two. Never mind,' said Preston. 'That isn't important. But eighty-three years is a long time. You must have learned something since they came. The Gates,' he urged. 'Surely you must know something about the Gates.

'Yes,' said Sylvia. 'We do. We know all about them. That,' she added, 'is why we rescued you.'

★ ★ ★

A bell chimed softly, and John looked at the clock. The hands pointed to 5:15. 'Second shift coming up,' he said quietly. 'We haven't got much more time.' Preston asked him why. 'We've got things arranged,' he said obliquely. And then, to the girl. 'What about it, Sylvia? Do we go ahead or wait some more?'

'Wait for how long?' She made a negative gesture. 'We've got to take this chance while it's going. At least we can trust him.'

'Would someone,' asked Preston, 'mind telling me what all this is about? I've got an interest,' he added. 'I take it that you intend to use me for some purpose of your own. Am I right?'

John nodded. 'You object?'

'You're damn right I object,' said Preston bluntly. 'I want to know what I'm getting into. And,' he added, 'I want to know what's in it for me.'

'We saved your life,' said the man. 'Isn't that worth something? Loyalty, perhaps?' He looked at the woman. 'I don't like this,' he said. 'He's too mercenary. He could sell us out.'

'You're crazy,' said Preston disgustedly. 'Amateurs,' he said. 'Part-time conspirators. So you saved my life, all right, I'm thankful. But don't expect me to be so grateful that I'll do anything you say. You tested me,' he pointed out. 'You know that I'm safe to trust. If you can't believe in your own findings then why are we here?' He looked at the woman. 'You said that you know all about the Gates. Do you mean that literally?'

'Yes.'

'You know how they work? How to build them?'

'Yes.'

'Then why the hell haven't you done it?' Preston knew the answer. 'You can't. You haven't the technology. You've concentrated on the medical sciences and relied on the Kaltich to supply everything

198

else. You're like an aborigine who is told exactly how to manufacture a radio. To him the knowledge is useless because he doesn't know how to even get started. How to mine ores, extract metals, grow transistors. But you're intelligent,' he said. 'The analogy isn't exact.'

'It's close enough,' said John. 'What you say is true. We've learned how to build a Gate but we don't know how to build the components. Even if we did we still haven't the scientists to understand the theory. That's where you come in.'

'Just a minute,' said Preston. 'One thing at a time. How did you get this information?' he asked the woman. 'The Kaltich would never have given it to you.'

'We stole it. From the minds of those who came here for treatment,' she explained. 'A little at a time. The basic theory from one, the structure from another, the circuitry from the third. It took more than fifty years. We aren't clever,' she admitted. 'Not in the field of electronics and atomics. For two hundred years we've concentrated on medicine to the exclusion of almost everything else.

But we knew that we had to become independent of the Kaltich. So we probed minds, a thousand, ten thousand minds. They guard the secret well. But, slowly, we've learned how it can be done.'

The bell chimed again. Preston ignored it. 'What do you want from me?'

'You've travelled from world to world,' said John eagerly. 'Aside from the Kaltich you're the only one we know who has done so. You could take the secret of the Gates and go to a world which has the technology to build them. In return you supply us with operating Gates.' He took a deep breath. 'Then,' he said slowly, 'we can get rid of the Kaltich for good.'

'My world could build them,' said Preston confidently. I'm not lying, he thought. Any race that can jump from steam to atomic power in the space of a single lifetime could do damn near anything if they had the incentive. And if these people could give me the plans?

He rose, too excited to remain seated, pacing the floor as he thought about it. He'd set out to get two things and one of them was almost in his lap. Two?

'You make the longevity treatment here,' he said slowly. 'You could tell me how it's done. Give me the plans of the machine.'

Sylvia frowned. 'Machine?'

'That's right,' said Preston. 'You go to a Gate,' he explained. 'Old people, that is. They get tested out on a machine and then get the treatment. If the Kaltich allow them to have it,' he said, remembering. 'If you cross them in any way they won't play. But you must know all this.'

'Maybe,' said John cautiously. 'What are you getting at?'

'When we start to make the Gates the Kaltich may learn what we're doing. If they do they'll crack the big whip. They'll stop giving the longevity treatment. Our governments are composed of old men,' he said. 'Do I have to draw you a picture?' He looked at their blank faces. 'I've got to weaken the Kaltich all along the line. If I've the secret of the longevity machine then I've got them where it hurts.'

'It isn't a machine,' said the woman slowly. 'It is a balanced injection of certain semi-intelligent organisms which are capable of recognizing degeneration and rectifying it. Like a gang of builders,' she explained. 'Send them to an old building with suitable materials and they will renovate the place. You couldn't manufacture the serum,' she insisted. 'Even if we told you how to do it.'

'And we're not going to tell you,' said John flatly. He was shrewd, thought Preston. No fool. Maybe he'd made a mistake in trying to grab too much but the chance was one he'd had to take. 'You get the gates built and supply us with them. In return we'll supply all the serum you need. In fact,' he added, 'that can be a part of our bargain.'

'The formulae too?'

'Yes,' said the man. 'You have my word for it. The word of GERM.'

Preston snapped his fingers. 'That's another thing,' he said accusingly. 'GERM. General Earth Resistance Movement. Earth. Why Earth?'

Sylvia frowned. 'Why not?' she said. 'What else should we call ourselves? This is Earth, isn't it?'

'No,' said Preston. 'How can it be?

Earth is my world.'

'And ours,' said John. He looked at Preston. 'Let's get this straight,' he demanded. 'Just what do you think the Gates are?'

'Matter transmitters,' said Preston. 'Space warps, how the hell should I know? But you step into them on one planet and step out on another.' Both shook their heads. 'No?'

'There's only one planet,' said Sylvia. 'This one. This is all of it. We learned that from the Kaltich but we'd have known it anyway. From the specimens they send us,' she explained. 'From the patients. From the Kaltich themselves. They're too similar. Coincidence couldn't stretch so far. Surely you must have wondered why the Kaltich are physically so human?

'There's only one planet,' she insisted, not waiting for an answer. 'And this is it. Earth.'

12

Preston closed his eyes and saw a gigantic book filled with an infinity of pages and each single page was Earth. The same planet circled the same sun but each page bore a slight modification. Earth — when the dinosaurs had continued to rule and mammals had failed to appear; when the ice still reached almost to the tropics; when the sun had entered a zone of dust and the seas had frozen; when Gondowanaland still reared above the waves; when Roman Legions still held their empire.

An infinity of Earths each a fraction different from the other, but those fractions accumulating until the planet became hardly recognizable. Hadn't been recognizable. Aside from one, he thought. The first. The place with the Red Indians and the buffalo. In that Earth, perhaps, the Spanish hadn't discovered Mexico. Or the Pilgrim Fathers had never reached

New England. Or there had been no war of Independence. Or . . .

Infinity was all there was and could be. Name it and it was included.

Preston sighed and eased his aching head. The concept hadn't caused the pain. He glared at the instrument standing against one wall of the little room. Hypnotism, he thought, should be painless. But this wasn't the mild suggestion he had known. This was something far more vicious and far more efficient. A teaching device perfected in this particular Earth. In his brain, waiting to be summoned, were the full facts concerning the Gates as learned from the reluctant Kaltich. Sylvia had told him that, and he had no reason to doubt what she said. He looked at the clock. 16:54. Ten hours, he thought. High speed tuition. Forced planting of reams of information. Plans, circuits, composition of alloys, relationships of components — it would all come out, so she had said, at the proper time.

In the meantime his head felt about to burst.

He rose, searched the room and found nothing to drink. He tested the door and found it locked. Nice, he thought. They leave me here, locking me in, taking their damned treatment and they can't even bother to let me have an aspirin.

Back in the chair he brooded on what he had discovered. Alternative worlds — why hadn't anyone thought of that before? Because no one but the Kaltich were allowed through the Gates. The Kaltich and a few selectees who never returned. They supplied cells for the growth of spare parts and then, he guessed, were sent somewhere else. But never back to their home world. Logical, he thought. And clever. Damned clever. They let us make the obvious mistake and so guarded their secret. And they didn't lie, he admitted. Not really. What else could they call the alternate Earths but other worlds? And some of them must be empty, virgin of human life, a paradise waiting to be filled.

A warp, he mused. The Gates had to be that. Some twisting of probability so as to penetrate the barrier between what was and what might have been. Not space travel but something even better. An endless supply of habitable worlds. Pick one and skip a thousand. No point in dealing with exactly the same cultures. Not enough Kaltich to do it, perhaps. They would have to be spread pretty thin as it was. The ruling castes at least. And it explained the language. Galactic, he thought. Well, it was easier for a thousand races to learn one language than for one race to learn a thousand.

Again he rose and tried the door. It was still locked. He hesitated, wondering whether to force it open, then decided against it. He could do nothing but wait.

Traders, he thought. That's all the Kaltich were — the middleman with a monopoly of transport and the longevity treatment as a threat to keep their customers in line. Traders who set their own margins of profit and diverted a stream of wealth to their home world. There even the lowest epsilon must enjoy more luxury than a terrestrial millionaire.

Fifty years, he told himself. That's what Hilda Thorenson had predicted. Fifty years and we'll all be working for the Kaltich. Then what? The heads of government bribed with alpha red. Diplomats, tycoons, industrial magnates with beta yellow. Top management with gamma green. Junior executives and the professional classes with delta blue. The rest would wear white and like it. All but the inevitable segment who like to carry out the orders, do the dirty work. The ones who had no imagination. The sadists. The concentration-camp guards. The blank-faced, blank-minded people who loved petty authority.

Earth would provide its own nulls.

★   ★   ★

The door clicked and John entered the room. He smiled as Preston winced and offered a bottle. It contained a clear liquid. Two hundred proof alcohol, Preston decided after he'd taken a cautious sip. He took another, the liquid seeming to evaporate in his mouth. Suddenly his headache was gone. 'You took your time,' he said, handing back the bottle. 'I was about ready to tear open the door.'

'I had to wait until it was safe,' said the man. He had, Preston noticed, changed from nondescript grey into orderly's pink. He carried a bundle which he put down on the table. 'The place is swarming with Kaltich,' he explained. 'They even had their own physicians examine your body. The one that took your place, that is.'

'And?'

John shrugged. 'I just work here. As long as they can't prove anything we've nothing to worry about.' He grinned as Preston reached for the bottle. 'Hypno-teach can be rough,' he said. 'There was a lot to squeeze in and little time to do it but we had to work fast. We still have to. My guess is that the Kaltich will be making a head-count and null-check of the entire building. We've got to get you out of here before then.'

Preston took another sip of the white lightning. The evaporated liquid seemed like a cooling breeze on the surface of his brain. 'How are you going to do that?'

'We'll use an emergency Gate. We've

managed to fix things so that, at a certain time, the operator will be alone. That's when we move in.' He reached out, took the bottle, helped himself to a drink. 'Clothes,' he said. 'I guess those you're wearing wouldn't do at home?'

'No,' said Preston.

'I've got you some others. Kaltich gear. Made up from uniforms which should have been burned but somehow weren't. What colour would you like?'

'Red,' said Preston immediately.

John shook his head. 'We could have made you a facsimile but it would never pass you through the Gate,' he said. 'Alpha uniforms carry a wire-pattern for purpose of identification. You could wear a stolen one but you wouldn't get far. Not alone.'

Not even with company, thought Preston. 'Yellow?'

'Betas are much the same. We settled for green. It's common enough so that you should get by, not so common that it doesn't carry enough weight.' John handed Preston the package. 'Green,' he said. 'I'm glad we could agree.'

'A comic,' said Preston sourly. 'You

must come and visit me one day.'

'The sooner the better.' John glanced at the clock. 'Get changed now. We haven't much time.'

The uniform, at least, fitted better than the others he had worn. Preston adjusted it, slipping the loop of the whip over his wrist, wondering what colour he would be wearing next. White, probably. The colour of a shroud. He followed the GERM agent from the room and along the passage leading to the spare-part banks. The place seemed as deserted as before. Timing, he thought. Cooperation. Plan things right and a man can stay invisible in a crowd.

'Every Gate is connected to one or other of these banks,' said John. Preston guessed that he was making conversation to steady his nerves. That, or it was a part of the camouflage. To a spy ear monitor he would appear to be a guide conducting one of the Kaltich on a tour of the basement. 'A one-way connection from us to them. They are in touch by phone. An order comes in, is phoned through to us, we fill it and pass it through the Gate. A small Gate,' he added. 'None of the packages are large.'

Information, thought Preston. He's using the time to fill me in. 'How do you get paid?' he demanded. 'Credit?'

'That's right. We use it to buy whatever we need.'

From the Kaltich, of course, thought Preston. They had it made both ways.

John slowed as they came to an open space. Messengers sat on long benches facing a row of hatches each with a signal light and phone. Other hatches, wider, without lights or phones stood opposite. Orderlies in bright pink could be seen at the openings. The place reminded Preston of the dispatch section of a department store.

John slowed still more, idling, killing time. He halted as a light winked above one of the hatches. Immediately a messenger ran to it, picked up the phone, listened, wrote something on a pad. Tearing off the slip, he went to one of the larger hatches and handed it to the orderly. Thirty seconds later he received a package, checked the number and returned.

Through the small Gate Preston could see a man in white, an epsilon, standing in a small room. He had seen such a room before at the New York Gate but this time he was seeing it from the other side. The messenger threw the package through the hatch and returned to his bench.

Another heart, thought Preston. Or a new pair of lungs, or a kidney, a spleen or maybe a new stomach. He looked along the line of hatches, counting them, multiplying them by how many? A hundred? A thousand? More?

'Come on,' said his guide.

He led the way past the line of hatches, turned a corner and halted before a closed door. He opened it and stepped through, closing it as Preston followed. A soft humming and the scent of ozone filled the air. A second door faced the first, yielding as the orderly used a glittering instrument. The agent eased it open a crack and produced an aerosol can fitted with a short nozzle. He slipped the nozzle through the door and pressed the release.

'All right,' he said. 'We can go in now.'

Inside a solitary gamma sat before a

complex instrument panel. The double arch of a Gate yawned to one side but neither had been activated.

'Emergency communicator,' said John. He ignored the Kaltich who sat, eyes open, staring at nothing. Instantaneous knockout gas, Preston decided. No warning and no after-effects. The man would come to full awareness and not realise that time had passed.

'All right,' said John, studying the controls. 'Where to?'

'Earth,' said Preston without thinking. The GERM agent swore.

'We've no time for games! I know it's Earth — but which one?'

I don't know, thought Preston wildly. Damn it. I don't know!

Take a number, double it, multiply it by your age, take away the number you first thought of. That way you had as much chance to be right as any other. From one to which? Not one, thought Preston. At least he knew which that was. The Kaltich home world. The last he wanted to visit.

'Quick,' said John impatiently. 'We've

got maybe another ninety seconds before the gas wears off. I want to get you out of here before then. I want to get out myself too,' he added. Then seeing Preston's expression. 'What's the matter?'

'I'm lost,' said Preston, and explained. 'What number is this world?'

'2360. Why?'

'A thought.' Semmelweis was known here, a hero. The divergence could have occurred about then. In this world he'd been hailed as almost a messiah. In Preston's own he'd suffered violent derision. But even so what did that prove? How many alternatives lay between?

'Come on,' said John. 'We haven't got much longer.'

'I don't know,' said Preston. 'Damn it, man, can't you understand? I don't know.' We never considered the problem, he thought. Earth should have been good enough. How the hell was I to guess that every damn planet would have the same name? 'Listen,' he said. 'This is the control, right? Well there should be a book of some kind. A directory. A list of worlds and their numbers.'

'Why?' asked John.

'Damn it, don't be so stupid!' Preston fought to remain calm. The obvious, he thought. How many plans have failed because someone overlooked the obvious? 'Look at it this way,' he said. 'I'm an alpha. I want to go to the world of living crystals but I can't remember or never knew the number. Is the operator supposed to know? From memory? How many worlds could he remember anyway? And with an alpha you don't take chances. Send him to the wrong place and you'd wind up under the whip. There must be such a book,' he insisted. 'For Pete's sake let's find it!'

He began to search the place, looking for cabinets, drawers, anywhere which could serve as a repository for the essential information. The agent swore as he glanced at his watch.

'This is getting us nowhere. Keep calm,' he said as Preston started to protest. 'I've got a better idea.' He dug into his pocket and produced another container of chemicals. 'Hypnogas,' he explained. 'For emergencies, but I didn't want to use it. The after-effects,' he said. 'Minor but obvious. But it looks as if we've got no choice.' He looked at his watch again. 'I'll have to wait until he recovers. Let's hope his associate doesn't return before then.'

'Lock the doors,' said Preston.

'Lock — but why?'

'Do it! You can, can't you? Then do it!' The gamma stirred as John returned from sealing the panels. Hastily he applied the hypnogas. 'I still can't see why you wanted me to lock the doors. It'll cost me time getting out.'

Preston ignored the agent. He stared at the operator who sat, unresisting, in his chair. 'Listen,' he snapped. 'I want a world which has a fairly high technology. One which has the use of atomic power but not space flight. Forget the atomic power,' he added. Could you call bombs atomic power? A scatter of indistinguishable power plants? 'A world that has extensive air travel,' he compromised. 'Heavily populated. Hurry!'

The operator moved sluggishly, reaching for buttons. Light flickered from a panel. '1352, sir?'

'I'm not sure. Can you check? Are there photographs?'

The operator pressed more buttons. A screen flashed into brilliance. Preston stared at the unmistakable shapes of the pyramids. They proved nothing.

'The western hemisphere,' said Preston. 'The eastern seaboard of North America. New York. A city on the fortieth parallel.' He grunted as a familiar sight came into focus. 'That's it!'

The GERM agent leaned forward. 'Are you sure?'

'That's the Statue of Liberty,' said Preston. 'I'd know it anywhere.' He tensed as someone hammered on the inner door. 'I thought I told you to lock them both?'

'I did. I — '

'Connect the Gate,' Preston snapped at the operator. He waited, watching as the man set his controls. It was a matter of pressing buttons, of waiting until signal lights flashed exact synchronisation. Automatic, decided Preston. It would have to be. Each Gate must contain a computor and each panel must be the same.

'Connected, sir,' said the gamma dreamily.

'Thank you,' said Preston, and slammed the edge of his stiffened hand hard against the nape of the man's neck. He looked at the white face of the agent. 'Get into his clothes.'

'You killed him! You — '

'Get into his clothes!' Preston began to tear at the uniform. 'The Gate is probably rigged,' he snapped. 'It must register every operation. There could even be cameras. Someone is standing outside the door. What chance do you think you've got of escaping? None,' he said. 'You haven't the chance of a snowball in hell. You've got to come with me.'

'I can't do that! GERM — '

'That's why,' interrupted Preston savagely. He flung the gamma's uniform at the agent. 'If they catch you they'll suck you dry. You'll all be caught. Sylvia, think of her if no one else. Would you like to see her flogged with a Kaltich whip?' He swore as the banging on the door grew louder, heavier. It ceased and a spot on the metal grew cherry red. 'Hurry!'

John hesitated. 'I could use the gas,' he suggested.

'Hurry!' yelled Preston. 'Before they burn through the door.' His face was a snarling mask of animal rage. 'Or do I have to kill you too?'

★   ★   ★

They stepped through the Gate as the door began to sag, escaping one danger to face another, walking from the room into the familiar expanse of a main Gate. Preston resisted the impulse to run, walking quickly with the agent at his side, two gammas intent on their own business. A face looked from the booth and Preston lifted his hand, the whip dangling from his wrist. Act natural, he told himself. You're too busy to stop and talk but not too ignorant to ignore a member of your own class. The gesture seemed to satisfy the operator who ducked back into his cubicle. Ahead lay the ramp, the unloading bays, the big outside.

Preston caught his companion's arm.

'Steady,' he warned. 'Not too fast. Just keep walking and look straight ahead.'

John swallowed. 'My back,' he said. 'I can feel the bullets.'

'That would be a kindness.' Preston felt himself relax a little as they reached the far end of the ramp. Some epsilons were busy at the conveyor belt and a couple of nulls stood casually on guard. 'They won't shoot us,' he said. 'Not if they can catch us.' He tensed as he heard a shout from behind. 'All right,' he snapped. 'Let's see how fast you can run!'

They had left the central opening of the Gate and the open space was before them. Preston turned sharply to the left and raced from the building. He heard more shouts, louder, veered as something hummed past his head. Beside him John raced slightly ahead. Their shoes made soft, thudding noises on the turf. Preston looked back. Two nulls were chasing after them, heads down, elbows tucked into their sides. The late sun threw their shadows in grotesque elongation.

'Damn!' John swore as he stumbled and almost fell. Preston looked past him, at the white faces of watching people, at buildings, narrow streets. The perimeter was marked with a broad band of white. He could see no guards.

He veered again as they crossed the edge, yelled to the agent as he forged ahead, led the way to where a street ran crookedly from the Gate. Panting, his heart thudding, face streaming with perspiration, Preston ducked down the first intersection, crossed the street, ducked down an inviting alley. A trash can gonged as he stumbled in the gloom. Exhausted, he fell into a deep doorway and waited, ears strained for sounds of pursuit.

Beside him John fumbled in his pockets. 'I've got the gas,' he whispered. 'If they find us, get close — '

Preston nodded, lacking breath to speak, lacking strength to do anything but fight for air. Footsteps passed the end of the alley, hesitated, returned.

'Down here,' said a voice.

'Are you sure?' His companion was doubtful.

'There are shadows. They could be in a

doorway. Behind the trash cans even. Come on.'

Preston tensed, hand falling to his whip. I might get one of them, he thought. If I'm quick enough and lucky enough. But never both. I'm too beat for that. 'That gas,' he whispered to John. 'How far will it travel?'

'A few feet.'

It would have to do. 'All right,' breathed Preston. 'I'm going out. Spray when you get the chance.'

He stepped from the doorway, hands lifted to shoulder height, halting when he saw the two nulls. As he had guessed from their footsteps they were about twelve feet distant. They froze when they saw him, guns levelled.

'Don't shoot,' said Preston quickly. He stepped forward, then sagged, a man obviously at the limit of his strength.

'Where's the other one?' A null stepped closer. 'Answer! Where is he?'

Preston gestured with his whip. 'Down there,' he mumbled. 'I couldn't keep up. Just had to rest. I — ' He broke off, gasping.

'Don't move!' The nulls came closer, their eyes watchful, manner suspicious. Preston sagged a little more, swaying as if he was about to fall. A null stepped immediately before him. Reaching for the whip, he began to slip the loop from Preston's wrist. Preston dropped his other hand down to the null's gun and pushed it aside as he fetched up his knee. The gun exploded as the man doubled in pain.

'You — !' The other null jumped back, gun lifted, knuckle white on the trigger. Preston fell, clawing at the gun in his victim's hand. He gained it as something dark ran from the doorway. A gun barked once, twice.

Preston fired the third shot. The null slumped, a hole between his eyes. John groaned as he tried to stem the gush of blood from his stomach.

'You damned fool!' Preston lifted the man's head. 'Why didn't you use the gas?'

'I tried. The range was too far. Not much good in the open.' The GERM agent coughed. 'You'd better get moving,' he gasped. 'Don't worry about me.'

Preston stooped, lifted the man, sweating beneath the strain.

'Don't!' The cry was almost a scream. 'You can't help me. Put me down! Damn you! Put me down!' John coughed again as he sagged on the concrete. 'Get moving you fool! Run! Don't let everything we've done go to waste!'

Preston took a deep breath. Rising, he looked towards the end of the alley. People, civilians, were gathered into the opening. Vultures, he thought. Attracted by the sight of blood, the aura of violence. They wore sober clothing and were probably harmless but, harmless or not, they would draw the attention of others.

He stooped, scooped up a gun, looked at John. The man had his eyes closed in the repose of death. 'Goodbye,' said Preston. And ran.

Ten minutes later he halted and wiped the sweat from his face. There was no sign of pursuit and he doubted if there would be. He had penetrated too deep into the city, was too far from the Gate. For the first time he had the chance to look around and orient himself.

The city wasn't New York.

At least it wasn't the New York he knew. He tilted his head searching for a familiar skyline. His knuckles whitened as he gripped the whip. He couldn't recognize anything he saw.

13

Chung Hoo sat at his desk and studied a graph. It was a simple thing and because of that carried no obvious threat or terror, but to anyone with imagination the two lines, one red and other green, spelled out a sickening message. The population was increasing faster than the total food production. Too fast. Every tick of the clock someone, somewhere, was dying of literal starvation.

But with every tick of that same clock how many new mouths came yelling into the world? A hundred? More? One would be one too many.

The handwriting on the wall, he thought, looking at the graph. The message any schoolboy had the intelligence to understand but which we've ignored for too long. Ignored because politicians aren't schoolboys. Pushed to one side for later solution. There has to be a solution, he told himself fiercely. One way or another the teeming masses of the world had to be fed. Fed, he thought bleakly, or reduced.

His intercom hummed. He pressed a button. 'Yes?'

'A visitor, sir,' said his secretary. 'Gamma Eldon of the Kaltich.'

'Send — ' The door burst open before he could finish. 'Never mind.' He rose to greet his visitor. 'Gamma Eldon, sire! This is a pleasure!'

'Not for me,' snapped the Kaltich. 'And I doubt if it will be for you.' He sat without waiting for an invitation. 'The patience of the Kaltich is close to exhaustion,' he said abruptly. 'We are on the verge of closing the New York Gate. Permanently,' he added. 'And there could be others.'

'The reason?'

'The utter lack of cooperation we have been receiving from the local authorities. And,' said Eldon savagely, 'by local I mean the authorities of this world. UNO, for example. The national services. Everyone.'

Chung Hoo sat down, thoughtful, his

face its accustomed mask. An upstart, he thought, looking at the Kaltich. A man enjoying a recent promotion. Wanting to throw his weight about, prove something to himself, perhaps. It was an unpleasant change. At first the Kaltich had been pleasant, persuasive, eager to make mutually satisfying arrangements. They were still persuasive, he thought. But now it was the persuasion of the whip.

'Let us be more precise,' he said. 'Are you speaking of the demonstration?'

'That and other things.'

'Such as?'

'A man named Martin Preston. An organisation known as STAR.' Eldon slashed his whip at the desk, the metal barbs scarring the carefully polished wood. 'You must know about them.'

'STAR is a group of fanatical idealists,' said Chung Hoo quietly. 'People of limited imagination. It amuses them to act as conspirators. But they have few members and little strength. They certainly do not have official backing.'

'Perhaps, perhaps not.' Again the whip slashed a scar on the wood. He's substituting, thought Chung Hoo. He really wants to send that lash across my cheek.

Quietly he said, 'I must ask you to be more explicit. I cannot guess what is in your mind.'

'I want every member of STAR arrested and interrogated,' said Eldon. 'We shall ask the questions. We have our methods,' he added. 'But you must conduct the arrests.'

'Why?'

'It is your job. You have the men, the facilities, the local knowledge of where these people are to be found.'

'I didn't mean that,' said Chung Hoo evenly. 'Why do you want to question them?'

'It is not for you to ask questions,' snapped Eldon. The whip made a third scar. 'It is for you to obey!'

Chung Hoo leaned back in his chair. Before him, on the desk, the warning graph hardened his resolve. 'No,' he said deliberately. 'I think not.'

'You defy the Kaltich?'

Act like a doormat, Nader had said,

and you'll be treated like one. 'Yes,' said Chung Hoo blandly. 'If to refuse to act as you dictate is to defy you then call it that. And,' he added gently, 'what do you intend doing about it?'

'The Gates will be closed. All of them!' stormed Eldon. 'The heads of your government will die — all the old and helpless will die. No more rejuvenation treatments,' he threatened. 'No more spare parts for replacement surgery. No — ' He broke off, looking at his host. 'You don't care,' he said wonderingly. 'You simply don't care.'

'That the old and ill and crippled will die?' Chung Hoo looked at the graph. 'No,' he admitted, 'I don't care. In a way you would be doing Earth a favour.'

'You must be mad! Insane!'

Perhaps, thought Chung Hoo. No politician should ever allow himself the luxury of true emotion. For a moment he was tempted to further indulge himself, then reluctantly put temptation aside. Too well he knew how quickly those in high places would throw him to the wolves. Continued life, to them, was of greater importance than planetary pride. And yet he had gone too far for a simple apology.

'We digress,' he said. 'But it is as well to clarify the position. You can, of course, rely on our full cooperation, but it would be helpful if we knew the full extent of the problem. We have laws,' he pointed out. 'There has to be a reason for such mass arrests and interrogations. If you could tell me a little more? You mentioned a name,' he hinted. 'Martin Preston. Could we, perhaps, start with him?'

Eldon ran the tip of his tongue over his bottom lip. His face was white, tense with strain and something else. Rage, thought Chang Hoo. Or could it be fear?

STAR, he thought as he listened. So they've finally managed to do it. This time they've gone too far. The fools, he told himself. The blind, stupid fools! To send a man in disguise through a Gate. To attack the Kaltich at a most sensitive time. STAR, he thought bitterly. Stupid Thoughtless Arrogant Reactionaries.

And Preston was one of the worst.

★　★　★

Eldon had travelled from the Gate in his own official car. It waited outside the UNO building in flagrant disregard of the parking regulations. The two nulls in attendance looked stonily at all who passed. A uniformed policeman walked by as if they and the car were invisible. Lou Wensle grinned. 'This,' he said, 'is going to be a slice of cake.'

His companion grunted for answer. The two men stood in the main hall of the building, looking at the waiting car through the glass doors. Both were dressed as policemen — a disguise which had the double advantage of commanding respect and obedience as well as allowing them to carry pistols in quick-draw holsters. A disguise which also allowed them to use those pistols without causing alarm. The public were always on the side of armed authority.

'You sure he's here?' Dan Marcey glanced to where the bank of elevators connected with the upper floors.

'I'm sure. We got the word and it's good. Five hundred units good.' He chuckled again. 'Big money,' he murmured. 'And plenty more to come.'

Marcey grunted, looking at the elevators. A signal light halted on its downward path, hesitated, moved on down without stopping. 'This could be him.'

'It could,' Wensle agreed. 'Let's go.'

Both men stepped forward as the elevator reached the ground floor. The doors opened, revealing a flash of green. Both men entered, blocking the door, crowding the Kaltich into a corner.

'Down,' snapped Wensle to the operator and then, to Eldon. 'Our apologies, sire. You are Gamma Eldon?'

'What is the meaning of this?' Eldon reached for his whip. 'How dare you!'

'Zanies are congregating outside, sire,' said Wensle quickly. 'They plan a demonstration. We suspect they may have guns. For your own safety, sire, we beg you to cooperate. Your car,' he added, 'is waiting in the basement car park.'

The elevator reached the lower floor. The doors opened. Eldon hesitated, relaxing as he caught a glimpse of familiar black.

'Please, sire.' Marcey had stepped outside as if to stand guard. 'Hurry before the zanies can figure out what we mean to do.'

'Yes,' said Wensle, no longer polite. His left hand dropped, catching the half of the whip. His right hand put the barrel of his pistol into Eldon's spine. 'Hurry before I blow you in half!'

It was, he thought, one of the smoothest snatch-jobs he had ever pulled.

* * *

Jim Raleigh slammed his hand down on the table careless of the bruising impact. 'You're mad,' he said. 'Stark, raving insane. What the hell do you hope to get out of it? A medal?'

Oldsworth coughed, saying nothing, his eyes bright and watchful over his handkerchief.

'Kidnapping the Kaltich!' Raleigh threw up his hands. 'Hiring gangsters to do it. How long do you think they'll cover up for you if questioned?'

'I deny it,' said Oldsworth. 'I deny everything.'

'That isn't good enough.' Bernard

King, his features as expressionless as ever, stared from where he sat at the table. 'Chung Hoo is no fool. How long will it take him to guess that his secretary was bribed to inform someone when Eldon came visiting? The call could be traced. All right,' he said. 'So it went to a phone in some dive or other. That isn't important. What is important is that STAR will get the blame. We're skating on thin ice as it is. This could finish us.'

'It could finish me,' said Jim Raleigh. 'Chung Hoo knows that I'm connected with STAR. He gave me the message. Eldon gets turned loose or else.' He drew a finger across his throat. 'Where is he, Harry? This thing has gone far enough.'

Oldsworth coughed again.

'Answer, damn you!' shouted Raleigh. 'Do you want to kill us all?'

Hilda Thorenson lit a cigarlet and watched the smoke as it drifted from the glowing tip. 'Let's be logical about this,' she said. 'The Kaltich has refused to give Oldsworth the longevity treatment. What is he supposed to do? Sit down and wait for death?'

'But — '

'He panicked,' she continued, not paying attention to Raleigh's attempt to interrupt. 'That, believe it or not, is about the only sensible thing he could have done. When you've nothing to lose, then you try anything, hoping that it might work. You kidnap the Kaltich. You offer to swap their lives for your own. You say to them 'treat me and your people go free.' Is that right, Harry?'

Oldsworth gnawed at his lower lip. His teeth were yellow, stained. He looked at his veined, shaking hands. 'Old,' he said. 'Dying. What the hell have I got to lose?'

'So you did snatch Eldon?' Raleigh was quick to the attack. 'You admit it?' He half-rose as if to grab the other man by the throat. 'Do you realise what you've done?'

Bernard King reached out and pressed him back into his chair. 'There's no need for us to be excited,' he said. 'This thing wants thinking out.'

'Go right ahead,' said Raleigh. 'What's stopping you? Just sit there and think it all out. And then what? I'll tell you,' he shouted. 'We can all forget staying alive. Our names will be at the head of the blacklist. Damn it, Oldsworth. You've killed us all!'

'Shut up!' snapped Hilda Thorenson. 'Stop being so selfish. You're blaming Oldsworth for doing exactly what you're doing now,' she pointed out. 'You're thinking of your own skin. Well, so is he.'

She drew at the cigarlet and blew a thin plume of smoke. 'You can't do it. It doesn't matter how many of their people you snatch, you still can't force them to give you what you want. Think about it,' she urged. 'And you'll see why.'

'The longevity treatment,' said Raleigh. He had calmed down a little and was using his brains instead of his mouth. 'It only lasts ten years. What happens then? More snatches? How long do you think they'd put up with it?'

'Score ten out of ten,' said Hilda Thorenson. 'Oh, they'd agree right enough,' she said to Oldsworth. 'They'd make a deal. They'd take you in and give you something. Poison,' she said. 'A slow-acting poison. Or they'd feed you a synthetic drug, one of the instant-addictives, or a malignant implant that will slowly eat away your nervous system. The one thing they won't do is to play square. They daren't. It would set a precedent.'

'I'll keep him,' said Oldsworth. 'Hold him until I'm checked out clear.'

The woman sucked at her cigarlet. 'Eldon is a gamma,' she said. 'Not an alpha. Not even a beta. Just a lousy gamma. Do you think the Kaltich will waste tears over him?'

'All right,' said Oldsworth, forgetting to cough in his rage. 'So I made a mistake. I'm going to pay. Well,' he said, 'if I am then so is that damned alien. I'll give him the treatment and send him back in a parcel. A small parcel.'

'No!' Raleigh was shocked. 'You can't do that! The retaliation — '

'We could maybe cover,' suggested King. 'Put the blame on the gangsters who did the job. STAR could even get the credit for rescuing him. The gangsters wouldn't talk,' he added. 'We could see to that.'

'That's a good idea,' admitted Hilda Thorenson. 'But I've got a better.' She crushed out her cigarlet and watched the ascending smoke. 'We'll keep him as a hostage,' she said. 'To help Martin Preston. Or have you all forgotten that he's out there somewhere working for us?'

★ ★ ★

Cherry Lee carefully finished applying the paint to her face and examined the result in a mirror. Ghastly, she thought, looking at her reflection. It scowled back at her, a demonic mask like a Maori's nightmare. The greased strands of her hair hung over her shoulders. She pouted at the mirror before turning away. She felt subdued, depressed, uninterested in what she had to do, ashamed of what she had not done.

I've failed, she thought. Chung Hoo trusted me to get close to Preston and I didn't do it. I waited too long. That doctor-bitch got him first, she told herself. Now he's in trouble and there's nothing anyone can do to help him out of it.

Trouble, she thought. The world contained nothing but trouble. She picked up the phone and punched a number. It was a visiphone. The screen showed a face as thickly painted as her own. The hair was roached in a high crest. 'Hi,' said the youth. 'Big Chief Quickfoot um ready to go on um warpath with big, fine squaw.'

'Be serious,' she said.

'I am serious.'

'Then act your age.' She added quickly, 'We've a special job on for tonight.' She told him what it was and he whistled.

'Search parties?'

'Unofficial,' she pointed out. 'Get the zanies to run over the neighbourhood. Have them check every cellar and basement. Clear the garages. I know it won't be easy,' she admitted. 'But we can do it without giving the alarm. We don't have to be vicious. Not this time.'

He scowled, thinking. 'Doesn't sound much fun,' he commented. 'How do we work it?'

'Make it an alien-hunt,' she advised. 'Get them steamed up about the Kaltich.

Pass the word that some may be hiding out and grab all you can find. Don't hurt them but run them back to the Gate.' Scare them to hell, she thought. Make them think twice about coming back into the city.

'I'll need some stuff,' he said. 'Something to fire the boilers.'

'Pick it up at the usual place. See you.'

She hung up the phone. Going to a drawer she took out a phial and swallowed a tablet. The euphoria was immediate but a low intensity. To the inside of her naked thigh she taped a thin, needle-pointed knife. A radio hung between her breasts. Carefully she sharpened and painted the fingernails of both hands with a solution containing a strong anaesthetic.

She felt restless despite the euphoriac, ill at ease.

Where is Preston? she wondered. What is he doing now? Why had STAR thrown another man to the Kaltich? Why the hell couldn't they see sense? Be reasonable, she thought, do it my way. Well, UNO knew the right way. If they didn't, who did?

The phone rang as she reached the door. Snatching it up, she saw the face of Chung Hoo.

'Hello, my dear,' he said in his gentle voice. 'Were you about to go out?'

'Yes,' she said. 'On duty.'

He nodded. 'I understand. But tonight your friends must do without you. I have other work for you,' he explained. 'Passage has been booked on the ICPM leaving Kennedy field within the hour. You will have to hurry.'

'Where am I going?'

'To Sheffield,' he said. 'A town in England. Martin Preston is there.'

14

At the library Preston was becoming something of a mystery. The woman in charge of the reference section, a romantic spinster who had waited too long for the right man, had her own theory. 'He's a student,' she said firmly. 'Brushing up before an exam.'

Her assistant, younger but more world-wise, shook her head. 'He's no student,' she said with equal firmness. 'Not in the way you mean. But he could be doing research,' she admitted. 'Perhaps he's an author?'

Oblivious of the exchange Preston sat and glowered at his books. They were all the library contained dealing with hypnotic techniques, forced tuition and compressed learning. None of them had helped. The information locked in his skull needed a key before it could be released. He had been trying to discover the shape of that key.

I'm wasting my time, he thought. I'll need drugs and the knowledge of how to use them. Relaxants and hypnotics so as to dig down deep. STAR will know exactly what to do. They'll get the experts and technical skill. He closed the book and leaned back in his chair. Around him the usual habitués of the reference section stirred and shifted on their hard seats. Old men seeking somewhere quiet to sit and dream. Young men hoping to gain affluence by study. A backwater in which strangers caused no comment.

His hotel was much the same. A small place but not so small that a stranger would stick out like a sore thumb and not so large that a stranger would be unnoticeable. Preston had taken time to select the right place. He halted at the desk. 'Any mail for me?'

'No, Mr Preston.' The receptionist was apologetic. 'No mail or messages.' She hesitated. 'There was someone asking about you,' she said. 'A man. I thought you would like to know.'

'Thank you,' he said. 'Did he ask after me by name?'

'Yes, sir. He said not to say anything. That he wanted to surprise you. But you are a guest of the hotel and I thought that you should know.'

'Thank you,' he said again. 'I appreciate you telling me.'

From STAR, he thought, walking from the desk. Or someone from the local police. They would have cause. He had left dead men lying in a London alley. He had stolen clothes, money, a suitcase, other things before catching the first monorail from the terminal. It had carried him to Sheffield. For two days now he had waited for STAR to get in contact.

Too long, he thought. Someone should have come sooner or at least sent him money. Now a man was asking for him. Asking about him, rather. An odd way for a friend to behave.

He slowed up going to his room, primitive instincts warning him of danger. His door was closed, locked, no light showing beneath the panel or through the keyhole. Cautiously Preston inserted his key into the lock and twisted. The latch moved back and the door eased open.

246

Taking out his key, he moved three steps down the corridor to the switch controlling the overhead lights. He turned it, plunging the passage into darkness. Softly he returned to his door.

Dropping to his knees he pushed it open. Nothing. Eel-like he slithered into the room. His right hand was tight around his gun he had taken from the null. A voice whispered from one corner.

'No need for all this caution, Preston. I'm from STAR.'

Preston didn't answer.

'I'm going to show my face,' said the voice easily. 'Just do me a favour and relax. I'm alone,' the man added. 'You've got nothing to be afraid of.' A cigarlet lighter spurted flame. A face covered with thin red lines of burst capillaries looked from beyond the flame. 'Daler,' said the man. 'Sam Daler. We've met before.'

'Yes,' said Preston. His hand moved, tucking the gun into his waistband, the butt hidden by his jacket.

'At STAR special rendezvous in New York,' said Daler. 'I was on lookout. You remember?'

'Yes,' said Preston again. His eyes searched the room. Daler was alone. He rose, snapped on the light, looked again. Stepping out into the passage he switched the overhead lights back on and returned to his room. Daler hadn't moved.

'Did you get it?'

Preston looked at the man. 'Get what?'

'What you went after.' Daler laughed without making a sound. 'I'm no wino,' he said. 'These lines — ' he gestured to his face — 'were caused by too-fast decompression when I worked the Maracot Deep. You went after something,' he said 'Did you get it?'

Preston ignored the question. 'Who sent you?'

'STAR. Who else? That's how I knew where to find you. King told me.' Daler lit a cigarlet number five size. 'What the devil made you come out in London?' he said. 'Why didn't you use the New York Gate?'

'I thought I was,' said Preston. 'The operator must have tricked me. I didn't specify,' he admitted. 'I just told him to connect. For a while I thought he'd sent

248

me to the wrong world. It was a ba
time.'

'The New York Gate was probably
engaged,' Daler said casually. 'It can
happen. Get your things together,' he
suggested, 'and we'll be on our way.'

'To where?'

'New York. I've got the flight times of
the ICPMs from London. Three hours
and we can be there.' Daler lifted his
hand to his inner pocket. 'I think we can
make it,' he said casually. 'I'll just check
on the times.'

'You do that,' said Preston.

And reached for his gun.

* * *

Chung Hoo walked in his garden and
indulged himself in the enjoyment of his
flowers. It wasn't a large garden and the
plants were confined to those which
would grow in pots and narrow boxes. In
fact it was the balcony of his living room,
beyond which Cherry Lee could see the
towering spires of skyscrapers, the dingy
canyons between.

missed him,' said Chung Hoo
That was most unfortunate.
iled,' she corrected him, 'again.'
o one can be infallible,' he said
itly. 'The blame is mine. I received the
iformation too late. You did your best,
my dear,' he soothed. 'You could have
done no more than what you did.
Preston,' he mused. 'A resourceful young
man. He has shown an amazing ability to
stay alive. Two shots, you say?'

'Yes. I had reached the hotel,' she said.
'I was that close. I was asking for him at
the desk when I heard the firing. Two
shots. I managed to be among the first to
enter the room. The man Daler was lying
dead. Preston had made his escape.'

'The police?'

'Did what they could but what did they
have to work on? A stranger killed for no
apparent reason.' She hesitated. 'Could
Preston have gone . . . I mean . . . ?'

'Crazy?' Chung Hoo picked up a
geranium and sniffed at the blood-red
blosom. 'No, my dear. I think that there is
a much simpler explanation. You traced
his activities?'

'He'd been using the local library. Reading all sorts of odd books. Technical books. I didn't take him for a scientist,' she said, frowning. 'Yet he'd been reading books only a scientist could understand.'

'There is an affinity between understanding and wanting to understand,' commented Chung Hoo. He delicately plucked a leaf from a marigold. 'Information is of no value unless it can be understood.' He moved to a snapdragon. 'Look at this,' he invited. 'See?' He demonstrated again. 'When you press the bloom, so, the petals gape open like a mouth,' and because the thought was constantly with him he added, 'a hungry mouth. Why did Preston kill?'

She knew the question to be rhetorical.

'Why does any man kill? For reasons of fear? Of hate? Of personal gain?' Chung Hoo sniffed a sweet pea. 'Daler,' he mused. 'An apparent drunkard attached to STAR. Or so we thought, but obviously we were wrong. An assassin perhaps? What did Preston discover which forced him to kill the man? Was he armed? Daler, I mean.'

'No,' she admitted. 'There was no obvious weapon, but what does that mean?' Flexing her fingers, she studied her nails. 'I could paint these with curare. A scratch would kill. Would I be carrying an obvious weapon? There was a stylo by his hand,' she said. 'A thick one. It could have been a projectile weapon of some kind.'

'It was,' he said blandly. 'I have received the report of the local police. But how did Preston know that Daler threatened his life? Know enough to draw his gun and shoot without hesitation?'

'And why should Daler want to kill him in the first place?' asked Cherry Lee.

Chung Hoo caressed a petunia.

'Reason,' said Cherry Lee. She realised that her employer was permitting her to work out something for herself. 'There has to be a reason. A man does not kill for fun. Not a man like Preston, at least. He could have been afraid,' she suggested. 'Shot in self-defence. But even so he must have suspected that Daler was after him. Wanted to kill him. But why?'

'Preston had recently returned through a Gate,' pointed out Chung Hoo. 'We can only guess what dangers he faced, what hardships he underwent while with the Kaltich. Violence must have been a part of his adventure. We know that he had to run for his life when he left the London Gate. But we speculate to no purpose. Preston himself could tell us all we wish to know.'

'If we can find him,' she said.

Chung Hoo smiled.

'You know where he is,' she accused. 'You've known all along. Where is he?' she demanded. 'Where?'

'With Hilda Thorenson,' he said quietly. 'Shall we join them?'

* * *

The swimming pool was the same, the sun, the naked luxury. The inflated duck still bobbed in the water, watching, but this time the woman wasn't nude. Red nylon held her curves in taut restraint, a barrier to passion, a promise of pleasures to come. Pleasures, thought Preston dispassionately. Things of the flesh. Bribes to buy a boy.

'I still can't believe it,' said Hilda Thorenson. 'You actually succeeded. Tell me.' She sat very close. 'Tell me all about it. Everything.'

Preston shook his head. 'First things first,' he reminded. 'There was talk of money. A lot of money.'

'Two million units,' she agreed. 'From Oldsworth. But he's dead.'

Preston raised his eyebrows.

'Killed,' she said. 'I don't know by whom.'

'From STAR then. I didn't work for nothing,' he insisted. 'The sum was agreed. One million for the secret of the Gates. Another for the secret of the longevity treatment. I can provide both.'

'To the highest bidder?'

'Perhaps.'

'Sell the secrets to me. I will give you the two million. Three, if you like.' Her voice was tense with excitement. She moved like an animal, the golden hairs of her body shining in the sun. The velvet of her pelt covering fat and muscle and brain shifted, begged to be touched, to be kissed. 'I helped you,' she pointed out. 'I

254

told you what to do. You owe me your success.'

He looked at her, his face bleak. 'How old are you?' he demanded. She smiled into his face. 'I want to know,' he insisted. 'How many years did you study to become a surgeon? How many years to gain practice? And,' he added, 'where did you obtain your degree?'

'The medical school of California,' she said evenly. 'You can check.'

'I did.'

'Tell me about the Gates,' she said. 'I want to know.'

'You have a wonderful apartment here,' said Preston. 'I didn't know that you owned the building.'

'A company owns it.'

'And you own the company.' He looked at her. 'I checked that too,' he said.

'The Gates!' She was impatient. 'Tell me about the Gates!'

'It's in here,' he said, 'All of it.' He touched his skull. 'Locked in tight but ready to come out at the right time. Plans, details, circuits, everything. With our technology we'll be able to build the first Gate within a year. With our production facilities we'll be able to turn them out one a minute. More. The Kaltich,' he said, watching her eyes, 'are finished.'

'Not yet,' she said.

'No,' he agreed. 'Not yet. Not while I hold the information. Not when I can be killed.'

'Exactly,' said Hilda Thorenson. 'Martin, you are so right!'

Preston looked up as a roaring came from the sky.

The helicopter dropped to hover at the side of the pool. In the downdraught the inflated duck bobbed like a thing alive. The rotors slowed as Chung Hoo and Cherry Lee stepped from the cabin. A signal and it lifted to drone a waiting circle.

'Martin Preston,' said Chung Hoo. 'Believe me, it is a pleasure to see you. Allow me to introduce myself. Chung Hoo. A humble servant of all nations.'

'UNO!' snapped Hilda Thorenson.

Chung Hoo bowed. 'Precisely, my dear lady. So you see,' he said to Preston, 'you have nothing to fear.'

'Get off my roof,' said Hilda Thorenson. 'At once!'

Chung Hoo shook his head. 'I must remind you that UNO has precedence over the activities of STAR. We could, if you wish, make an issue of it. No? I thought not. You are being wise.' He turned to the girl at his side, demure in normal clothing, innocent with absence of paint. 'Preston, this is Cherry Lee.'

'We've met,' he said curtly.

He was thinner, thought Cherry Lee. His face more finely drawn, the eyes burning in their deep sockets. His mouth showed a certain relentlessness. He's matured, she thought. Become harder than what he was. Once he looked a killer and now he really is.

She looked at Chung Hoo. What does he intend doing? she wondered. Why are we here?

'The secret of efficient government,' said Chung Hoo to no-one in particular, 'is to let people believe that they govern themselves. Also,' he added, 'to let them do the things that are necessary of their own volition. Every age needs a crusade,' he mused. 'A cause. Yours, Preston, was gaining the secret of the Gates. Did you succeed?'

'Don't answer him,' said Hilda Thorenson quickly.

Preston nodded. 'I did.'

'And now you expect your reward.' Chung Hoo was bland as he spread his hands. 'There is nothing wrong in that. The labourer is worthy of his hire. UNO has sufficient funds and would be willing — '

'The information belongs to STAR,' interrupted Hilda Thorenson. 'We can extract if from his head. We can use it. We know how best to bargain with the Kaltich for the right to share their alternates. We — ' She broke off. 'That is — '

Preston slapped her across the face.

★ ★ ★

'I owe you that,' he said grimly. 'For the beating I took. Seven lashes of a major whip. For the interrogation. For being shot and killed. For having to watch a

258

friend die. And,' he added, 'for your latest attempt to murder me.'

'But — ' Cherry Lee fell silent as Chung Hoo clamped his hand on her wrist.

'Daler was your man,' continued Preston. The words were bullets fired from the guns of his anger. 'I called you, told you where I was, asked you to send me money. Instead you sent Daler. To kill me. But he was careless. I was already suspicious and I got him first. The Kaltich taught me that,' he said. 'To kill before getting killed. You bitch!' he stormed. 'You damned renegade!'

She whitened beneath his anger.

'You are fond of wearing red,' he said. 'Each time I've seen you you've worn red. A fault,' he pointed out. 'You're a Scandinavian blonde and red isn't the colour which suits you best. It makes you look like a tart,' he said spitefully. 'A cheap tart. But would an alpha think of that? Or,' he added, 'someone who'd been conditioned to believe that red was the prime colour?'

She glared at him like a cat. 'One day,'

she said thinly, 'I shall kill you. It will not be an easy death.'

'I've been killed,' he said, calmer now. 'I know what it is to die. To be tortured,' he added. 'And for what? So that you could test the security of the Gates. You must have laughed at STAR. Amateurs playing at conspirators, not realising that we were rotten with spies. UNO agents,' he said looking at Chung Hoo. 'Raleigh and maybe King. And what of the other side? The Kaltich aren't fools. They must have their own intelligence network. In a world with a technology as high as ours they wouldn't dare do otherwise. Locals eager and willing to work for them. Some of their own people. Like Daler, for example. He was careless. He knew how it was that I came through the London Gate instead of the one at New York. An accident, but I'm betting that it saved my life. And he was ignorant. He claimed to have worked the Maracot Deep. He may have done — but never in this world. But he thought he could afford to be careless. He'd been sent to kill me. To shut my mouth.'

Hilda Thorenson stirred where she sat at the edge of the pool. Her cheek showed the red welts left by Preston's fingers. She touched them. 'Surmise,' she said coldly. 'Lies.'

'Truth. You made a slip,' said Preston. 'More than one if you want to count. A moment ago you mentioned alternate worlds. Alternates, you called them. How did you know that?'

He waited for her answer, shrugged when none came.

'But that wasn't your biggest error. You found a delta, Leon Tonach. I took his place. You searched his mind for information but the one fact he must have known you didn't tell me. He knew the Kaltich travelled between alternate worlds. He must have known. That means you knew also. Why didn't you tell me?'

She rose, tall, beautiful, eyes blazing with contempt. 'You thing of filth! Yes, I am of the Kaltich. What do you intend doing about it?'

'Nothing,' said Preston. 'Nothing at all. You can be escorted to the New York Gate this very moment if you wish.'

'No,' said Chung Hoo. 'Not that. Not yet.'

'She won't go,' said Preston. 'I killed an alpha,' he said to the woman. 'You realize what that means? An alpha, the next thing to God. How do you think your friends will thank you for what you've done? You did do it, you know. If you hadn't sent me into the Gate that alpha would still be alive. It was luck,' he admitted. 'Good for me but bad for you. Very bad. The one thing you could never have predicted. You thought that I'd be trapped at the Gate. That I'd do all I could to get through and thus show up any weakness. That your people would catch me and deal with me as they did Lassiter. But an alpha died,' he said grimly. 'You will be blamed for his death. Would you like us to escort you to the Gate?'

★ ★ ★

Cherry Lee stared thoughtfully down at the penthouse as the helicopter climbed into the sky. 'What will happen to her?' she wondered.

Chung Hoo tucked his hands in the sleeve of his jacket. 'She will die,' he said calmly. 'Shot or killed in some other way by her own people. They dare not leave her at large.' he explained. 'She dare not go back to excuse herself. As Martin pointed out, a caste system such as that of the Kaltich must always punish those who injure a member of a higher caste.'

'But if she's an alpha?'

'She isn't,' said Preston. He shifted a little but not too much. The cabin of the helicopter was roomy enough but, somehow, Cherry Lee had managed to press herself hard against his chest. It was the most natural thing in the world to drop his arm around her shoulders. 'An alpha would never consent to physical work and Hilda Thorenson has had to work, and does work, really hard. She also allows limitation on her personal freedom and that's another thing no alpha would ever tolerate. She wears red, true, but only because of a subconscious desire to improve her status. She has money, agreed, but so has every Kaltich.'

'You know,' said Cherry Lee. 'I could

almost feel sorry for her.'

Preston remembered the seven lashes. 'I'm not.'

'What's going to happen now?' asked Cherry Lee. She moved, letting Preston's arm slip from her shoulders to her waist, pulling it tight with shameless abandon. 'Are you going to get the plans from his mind? Build the Gates?'

'Yes,' said Chung Hoo.

'Right away?'

'Yes.'

'How long will it take? Getting the plans, I mean.'

'A day. A week. I cannot be sure.'

'And after?'

'Paradise,' breathed Chung Hoo softly. 'For everyone.'

THE END

FIFTY DAYS TO DOOM
THE DEATH ZONE
THE STELLAR LEGION
STARDEATH
TOYMAN
STARSLAVE

We do hope that you have enjoyed reading this large print book.

Did you know that all of our titles are available for purchase?

We publish a wide range of high quality large print books including:
Romances, Mysteries, Classics
General Fiction
Non Fiction and Westerns

Special interest titles available in large print are:
The Little Oxford Dictionary
Music Book, Song Book
Hymn Book, Service Book

Also available from us courtesy of Oxford University Press:
Young Readers' Dictionary
(large print edition)
Young Readers' Thesaurus
(large print edition)

For further information or a free brochure, please contact us at:
Ulverscroft Large Print Books Ltd.,
The Green, Bradgate Road, Anstey,
Leicester, LE7 7FU, England.
Tel: (00 44) **0116 236 4325**
Fax: (00 44) **0116 234 0205**

Other titles in the
Linford Mystery Library:

THE VANISHING MAN

Sydney J. Bounds

Popular novelist and secret agent Alec Black is on an undercover mission on Mars. The Martian colonists are preparing for a major offensive against earth and someone is stirring up war-fever. Black must try to prevent it, or the whole system will be engulfed in atomic war. When Black finds himself shadowed by a man who, when confronted, vanishes into thin air, his investigation turns into his strangest case and very soon he's plunged into a dimension of horror . . .

TOYMAN

E. C. Tubb

Space-wanderer Earl Dumarest is on the planet Toy, hoping he'll get information on the whereabouts of Earth, his lost home world. But nothing is given freely there and he must fight in the Toy Games to gain the information he needs. He's forced to be like a tin soldier in a vast nursery with a spoiled child in command — but there's nothing playful about the Games on Toy. Everything is only too real: pain, wounds, blood — and death . . .

THE PREMONITION

Drew Launay

Nostradamus lives . . . in his descendant Michael Dartson. On a journey to the homes of his ancestors, a strangely bewitching woman shows him that the past is alive. Michael must experience the most traumatic moments of his forefathers' lives — rape, cannibalism, unspeakable violence. His infamous ancestor has set some terrible plan in motion — and Michael is only an instrument. The time is near. The horrors of the past are nothing compared to the evils of the future . . .

STARSLAVE

E. C. Tubb

On several settled worlds of the Earth
Confederation, towns had been destroyed
by attacking alien vessels. Captain Kurt
Varl was the only man to have fought
an alien ship and destroyed it — the
only survivor from a crew of thirty. He
must lead another ship and crew into
battle, knowing that as well as the alien
raiders, he faced the things that lurked
in limbo, existing in four dimensions
and capable of transforming humans
into things of screaming horror . . .

THE MISSING HEIRESS MURDERS

John Glasby

Private eye Johnny Merak's latest client, top Mob man Enrico Manzelli, has received death-threats. A menacing man himself, he pressures Johnny to discover who was sending them — and why. Then Barbara Minton, a rich heiress, disappears, and her husband turns to Johnny. Despite Manzelli's ultimatum — that Johnny should focus on his case alone — he takes the job. But that's before he discovers the fate of the first detective Minton hired. And more bodies are stacking up . . .